He'd been keeping notes on everything she'd said!

Tess flipped through the pages of Steve's notebook, remembering the questions he'd asked about her parents' marriage, the answers she'd given him.

She staggered back into an armchair with a clatter that made Steve start and wake up. A smile crept across his face. "I was just dreaming about you," he said softly, holding out his hand.

"Were you dreaming I'd discovered you keep secret notes on everything I say?"

She watched him stiffen while he tried to work out his reply and she knew she couldn't bear to hear the lies he might invent. He'd used her to get at her father. He'd even been prepared to make love to her to get what he wanted.

She flung the notebook at him and fled the room.

Books by Charlotte Lamb

A VIOLATION
SECRETS

HARLEQUIN PRESENTS

HARLEQUIN ROMANCE

These books may be available at your local bookseller.

Don't miss any of our special offers. Write to us at the following address for information on our newest releases.

Harlequin Reader Service
P.O. Box 52040, Phoenix, AZ 85072-2040
Canadian address: P.O. Box 2800, Postal Station A,
5170 Yonge St., Willowdale, Ont. M2N 6J3

CHARLOTTE LAMB

who's been sleeping in my bed?

Harlequin Books

TORONTO • NEW YORK • LONDON
AMSTERDAM • PARIS • SYDNEY • HAMBURG
STOCKHOLM • ATHENS • TOKYO • MILAN

Harlequin Presents first edition December 1985
ISBN 0-373-10842-7

Original hardcover edition published in 1985
by Mills & Boon Limited

CHAPTER ONE

'I'LL never get over it,' Dottie said in a low mutter as they hurtled down the corridors of Heathrow, laden with hand-baggage.

'You will,' Tess promised. Dottie always did.

'He's a rat, I could have curled up and died!'

'He's not worth bothering about, forget him,' Tess comforted as they got out of the bus and fought their way through a storm of wind and rain up the steps into the plane.

'I wish I was dead—dead and buried,' Dottie wailed.

'I wish it would stop raining,' Tess said, watching a woman's hat blow away across the tarmac while its owner screamed in fury.

'My hat! My hat!'

'A kingdom for my hat?' Tess couldn't help murmuring and was given a glare of blank amazement by the owner who was not amused. Nor was Dottie, who was staring at Tess, too, eyes rounded, because she hadn't even noticed the hat bowl away across the rain-lashed airfield, and found Tess's murmur quite bewildering.

'What *are* you talking about?' she asked as they made their way down the plane to their seats. Dottie gratefully stowed her wet raincoat and small case into the locker and watched Tess do the same while Dottie went on talking about the subject obsessing her. Dottie's heart was broken and Tess was sorry for her, although her compassion was under some strain by the time they were flying over France, their shadow following them on the ground thousands of miles below, a flat black aeroplane speeding over valley and hill, with Dottie giving a running commentary on the current state of her heart at every mile. She wasn't so much drowning in heartbreak as wallowing in it and Tess wasn't sure how much of her lament she could take. When the stewardess brought some food, Dottie shook her head, a look of disgust on her face, visibly recoiling from the thought of anything so gross and mundane. Tess refused too, smiling; partly to keep Dottie company and partly because she was on a diet and suspicious of the number of calories under the cellophane wrappings. They both had black coffee, though; and Dottie smoked a cigarette, screwing up her eyes to see Tess through the haze. All the while she continued to talk about the married man who hadn't told her he was married, an omission his wife had eventually corrected by arriving on Dottie's doorstep one day with his three children and a great deal to say about home-wreckers and shameless women. It had all been a tremendous shock to Dottie. Until that moment she had frequently told Tess she wasn't sure she really liked Howard, well, she liked him but was it serious? Suddenly, with Howard whisked back to the matrimonial home, Dottie's heart had broken. Howard snatched away was Howard suddenly ultra-desirable, it seemed.

'I never even suspected, you know,' Dottie said in a voice made hoarse by hours of complaint. 'I was a blind fool.'

Tess peered out of the window. 'We're landing,' she said unnecessarily as the aircraft hit the ground with a thud and continued to bounce all the way down the tarmac of Nice airport.

'He didn't look married,' Dottie insisted as they took a taxi to the villa which had been lent to them by Tess's brother.

'I don't know, there was something shifty about his eyes,' Tess said tentatively with an eye on Dottie's face in case it was too early to start pulling Howard to pieces. To her relief, Dottie looked struck.

'Yes,' she said slowly. 'There was, wasn't there? Now you come to mention it, his eyes were rather close together.'

'His nose was too big,' Tess added. 'And his ears were simply grotesque.'

'Huge,' agreed Dottie, becoming thoughtful.

'He looked like a slimmer version of Dumbo,' Tess said gleefully. She hadn't particularly liked Howard, as it happened, but she liked him a lot less now that she had had to suffer hours of Dottie's heartbreak over him.

'I'm going to forget him and have a good time,' Dottie said, cheering up. She looked out of the taxi window at the blue-hazed backcloth of mountains which lay behind Nice's theatrical sparkle. 'How much further is it to the villa?'

'A couple of miles—it's just outside Vence. There's some marvellous countryside around it;

the Loup gorge and the mountains take your breath away.'

'It's very good of Hal to lend us his villa. Does he manage to get over here to use it much himself? He's always so busy, I wouldn't have thought he'd want a holiday home.'

'Deirdre and the children spend the summer holidays there and Hal goes over from time to time, but Hal lets it when they don't want it. I think he saw it as an investment more than anything else. It has a swimming pool and is quite large; Hal charges an enormous rent in the season.' Tess grinned lazily at Dottie, her dark blue eyes bright with teasing. 'Don't look worried. He isn't going to charge us anything. I told you—the people who had booked it for this fortnight had to cancel. Hal was going to have some re-decorating done while it was empty but when I said I wanted to get away he offered to let me use the villa and he'll have the decorating done when we've left. It isn't urgent.'

'All the same, I still think he's wonderful,' Dottie said, as they drove through a small village, tyres screeching on the hair pin bend just outside it. They hardly had time to notice much; a scattering of white houses, a church, a war memorial and a bar flashing by in a minute. Dottie did notice the shop and her eyes lit up.

'I'm starving,' she said. 'Shouldn't we stop and buy food?' She hadn't eaten since Howard's wife appeared on the doorstep and this sign of returning life made Tess smile. Dottie's tragedies never lasted long.

'I'm not sure what there is at the villa—we'll wait and see. Hal usually makes sure that there are some staples; a few tins and cereals—rice, spaghetti, muesli—that sort of thing. In case of emergency, you never know when you might run out of something and find the shops shut. They do in France—for days on end. From lunchtime Saturday to lunchtime Monday you're unlikely to find many shops open. They take the weekend very seriously.' She grinned. 'Don't worry, there's a very handy shop near the villa, we get all our stuff from there.'

Tess had been at the villa in the spring, acting nursemaid to Hal's three children while he and his wife took a cruise to Norway. Deirdre had had a minor operation a month earlier, and needed a break from her lively offspring. She was a loving but slightly chaotic mother and couldn't quite cope with the maelstrom her children seemed to enjoy creating; when things got too much for her she usually screamed for Tess. Deirdre's mother disliked children and from the moment when she set eyes on her first grandchild had calmly informed Deirdre that she need expect no babysitting from *her*, which hadn't surprised Deirdre since she herself had rarely set eyes on her wealthy and indifferent parents and had spent most of her first eighteen years with a nanny and then at boarding school.

'How are we going to get about?' Dottie suddenly asked, having only just thought of the problem.

'There's a hire car waiting for us at the garage

in the village. I rang yesterday to see if one was available—Jacques has several hire cars for summer visitors. He promised to have one ready whenever we go and pick it up.'

'You're so efficient,' Dottie said, her expression between awe and resentful accusation. 'You think of everything.'

'I've been here before,' Tess dismissed coolly.

'Oh, look—orange trees,' Dottie broke out, excitement in her brown eyes. They were on a narrow, winding road with villas on either side of it, surrounded by gardens brilliant with bougainvillaea and tall cypress trees. On the slopes of the rocky hillside were a few rows of vines interspersed with the silvery dance of olive leaves.

'There's Vence now,' Tess pointed out and her friend stared up at the picturesque little town, an irregular pattern of red roofs and white walls, broken here and there by a square stone tower and the Romanesque walls of the Cathedral, a few white spires and the tapering darkness of cypresses rising against a blue sky.

Tess leaned forward and spoke in careful French to the driver who a moment later turned into a rough, unmade road on which they bumped and jolted for a short time, pulling up at last in front of a white-painted wooden gate. Tess jumped out and undid the gate, pushing it back to allow the car to enter the circular drive in front of the villa.

The driver got out, removed their cases from the boot of his taxi; worked out how much they owed him and watched Tess count out the franc notes into his tanned hand. Dottie wandered around the garden blissfully gazing at the white tubs of geraniums, the sheltered lawn, the lime tree and hedge of bougainvillaea. The taxi drove out of the gate and Tess turned to watch her friend wryly.

'Give me a hand with the cases,' she invited, taking out the key of the villa from her handbag.

'It's gorgeous,' Dottie enthused, hurrying to help her. 'The air smells of flowers.' She jumped, dropping the case she had just picked up, giving a stifled shriek.

'What's wrong now?' Tess enquired pushing open the front door.

'Something green ran up the wall—look, there it goes again, behind that creeper with the blue flowers.'

'Lizards,' Tess dismissed, carrying one of the large cases into the cool and shadowed hall. 'Dottie, do come on— there's a lot to do before we can get into our bikinis and swim and I'm dying to get into the pool. I'm baking hot and dead tired.'

Dottie followed her, bringing several cases. 'Lizards,' she told herself. 'Bright green lizards running up and down the wall.' She didn't seem sure whether she found the thought entrancing or horrifying, but then she looked around the stone-floored hall with its plain white-washed walls, hung with watercolours of local places, and she was distracted by new impressions. Tess walked to the right and up the open stone staircase leading to the first floor.

'No hand-rail, so be careful,' she warned. 'Come and choose your room—there are four, so you have plenty of choice.' Tess pushed open the first door on the landing and went inside, putting down her case by the bed. The shutters were closed and the room was dim and cool. Everything was spotlessly tidy. Hal and Deirdre had a friendly arrangement with a local woman who came in several times a week to make sure that the villa was in immaculate condition at all times.

'This is my room,' she told Dottie who hovered in the doorway, staring at the Spanish-style red and black coverlet on the bed and the fitted white wardrobe with the louvre doors.

'I love the decor,' Dottie admired.

'Yes, Hal picked bold colours for the furniture and fittings—and white walls throughout. It's so easy to redecorate; you just get gallons of white paint and splosh it on, and it's so sunny here most of the year—white walls look fabulous in sunlight, and you can hang pictures on them without any clash of colours.'

She was already talking to a vanished audience; Dottie was going from room to room exclaiming and hesitating.

'I'm going to wash and get into shorts and a T-shirt,' Tess called, and Dottie yelled back.

'Okay.'

Ten minutes later Tess was downstairs in the modern fitted kitchen looking out over the rectangular splash of blue swimming pool when Dottie clacked into the room in a brief pair of bright pink shorts, a white T-shirt and white canvas sandals with high cork heels. Tess had made some tea while she was investigating the contents of the larder and fridge. As she had expected there was a wide variety of tinned vegetables and fruit, some biscuits and cereals and some long-life milk. Earlier occupants had left odd packets of things; some currants, a few noodles and some tins of baby food.

'While we have a cup of tea I'll make a list, then we'll walk to the shop and see what we can buy there. What do you fancy for dinner? We'll probably get some salad—how about escalope of veal?'

'Fine,' Dottie said, pouring the tea and making a face over the taste of the long-life milk. 'I'm very hungry now, though—I think I'll have a bowl of muesli with some of those tinned peaches.'

'We haven't got time, we must get to the shop before they sell out of salad,' Tess said, but Dottie was already pouring milk on to a bowl of muesli and mixing it carefully into a sticky paste.

'I'll put this into the fridge until we get back. It isn't ready to eat yet, anyway. Do they sell fresh fruit at this shop? I love muesli with strawberries.'

'So do I. It's too hot to cook, anyway. We'll probably end up living on muesli and yoghurt and salad without going anywhere near that stove.'

'A lazy holiday,' Dottie said contentedly. 'Just what I need.'

They had both been working very hard to make a success of their Chelsea boutique having invested every penny they had in the stock. The leasehold shop belonged to Tess, who had bought it with a small inheritance from her grandfather, but Dottie's flair for fashion had dictated the style they were trying to capture, and the shop was a joint venture in every way. Tess was good at organising and Dottie was good at selling—they made a great team, and they had discovered a small, energetic woman of well over fifty whose burning desire to do something with her life before it was too late made her a very valuable member of their team. It was Sybil who was running the shop while they were away, she had almost shoved them out of the door, she couldn't wait to be in total charge of the business, even if only for two weeks!

'Sun, sea air and good food,' Tess said as they set off along the lane to the village.

'And no men!' Dottie said and Tess gave her a laughing look of incredulity.

'Oh, I mean it!' said Dottie and Tess said: 'Sure you do!'

The sun was burning down on their heads. They walked under the shade of over-hanging trees, their bare legs brushed with cool fern. Cicadas kept up their soporific music, a heat haze shimmered on the road ahead and on the white stone walls of villas behind trees. They heard the splash of someone leaping into a swimming pool, from one walled garden, and Tess sighed yearning for the feel of cool water on her overheated skin. The first thing she would do when they got back was change into a bikini and head for the pool.

The village street was narrow and almost empty: a dog lay, panting in the shadow of a shop blind, some men sat at the tables of the pavement café. They stared at the two girls—Dottie's warm curves in bright pink, Tess slender and small-boned in brief dark blue shorts and a clinging white tube top which left her shoulders and arms bare. 'I never want to see another man again as long as I live,' Dottie muttered fiercely as they squeezed into the small, crowded shop, between huge boxes of detergent and bottles of cooking oil.

'I've heard that before,' Tess said, selecting fruit with sharp-eyed expertise while the shop-keeper watched cynically. 'You pick the wrong guys, next time you might try . . .'

'A wimp,' Dottie said in disgust, dropping some cans of sardines into the metal shopping basket. 'That's what *you* always pick, isn't it? A nice, polite, nine-to-five man with an insurance policy, polished shoes and a vest under his shirt.'

Tess laughed, taking two long sticks of bread from the shopkeeper. '*Fromage, Madame?*' she asked, then glanced at the selection on offer. '*Chèvre, s'il vous plaît,*' she said because you couldn't always get goat cheese in London and she liked it occasionally. Looking at Dottie ruefully she said, 'At least he wouldn't turn out to be married.' Dottie made a gruesome face of wry admission.

It took them longer to get back to the villa because they were walking up-hill now with heavy bags of shopping dragging down their arms and slowing them up. When they finally got to the front door Tess juggled with her bags while she found the key and unlocked the door. As she walked into the shadowy hall she paused, frowning. The villa was designed on the open-plan style; from the hall you could see into all the other rooms downstairs. Tess's eyes skated around from room to room, they all seemed quite empty and she couldn't hear a sound, yet she felt a strange prickling running down her spine, an instinctive frisson of alarm for which there was no reason.

The air seemed to her to vibrate—as though someone had just been in the house a moment ago and the sound of their breathing still hung on the air.

'What's wrong?' Dottie asked, puzzled.

'There's someone here,' Tess whispered, tiptoeing to the foot of the stairs and listening intently.

'What?' Dottie dropped the bags she was carrying and a jar in one of them clattered. Several oranges rolled out and Tess absently fended them with her foot.

'Ssh,' she mouthed at Dottie who crept over to join her. They both stared upwards then Dottie looked at Tess and said in a soft voice, 'I don't hear anything.'

'Maybe I'm imagining it,' Tess said, relaxing, then she saw that her bedroom door was wide open, and she stiffened again. 'Hey, didn't I close my door when I came out?' she thought aloud. 'I know I did, I remember. Did you go in there, Dottie?'

'No,' Dottie said nervously, her huge dark brown eyes opening wider and the curling lashes flickering rapidly in agitation. Tess dumped the two carrier bags she was holding into Dottie's arms and went over to the umbrella stand beside the front door.

'What are you going to do?' Dottie whispered as Tess selected a heavy gold-headed cane which her father must have left here during one of his visits.

'We've got to check it out,' she murmured. 'You stay here. It could be only Madame Beringer, come to do some housework.'

'Why not just call out?' Dottie anxiously suggested, backing, clutching the shopping.

'And have half the portable valuables vanish? Hal would never forgive me. There are radios and pictures up there—none of them are worth a fortune but Hal wouldn't want to lose any of them all the same. Insurance doesn't cover sentimental value.' She set a foot on the lowest stair and Dottie watched from a safe distance. Tess took it slowly, stair by stair, listening. There was a whirring sound and Dottie gasped in shock, then an Austrian cuckoo clock in the kitchen began to cuckoo and Tess got the giggles at Dottie's expression. She waited to move until it had finished. Four o'clock and all's definitely not well, she thought, edging her way up to the landing. The clock had been a present to Hal's children several years ago which had driven their father mad until he banished it to the holiday home; she understood his feelings.

She advanced gingerly into her bedroom, glancing around. The shutters had been opened, she saw at once, and then she saw something else—someone had been lying on her bed. The Spanish coverlet had a clear impression of a long body; she could see where the head had been laid on the pillow and where the feet had dug into the far end of the bed. Tess pushed the gold-headed cane under the bed and swung it about. It didn't hit anything. She opened the wardrobe, on the alert in case anyone leapt out at her. A minute later she was quite sure that the room was empty. She went through the other rooms just as methodically while from below Dottie hissed from time to time, 'Tess ... Tess ... where are you?'

Satisfied that nobody was upstairs, Tess came down, the cane over her shoulder as if she meant to break into a song and dance routine at any minute.

'Well?' quavered Dottie.

'Not a sign of anyone except that someone has been sleeping on my bed,' Tess said. 'And it wasn't Madame Beringer—she's short and distinctly round. This was a man, I'd say; over six foot tall and not heavy, with black hair and rubber-soled shoes.'

Dottie's mouth satisfyingly dropped open. 'Are you kidding?'

'No, Watson. I found a black hair on the pillow and the imprint of a rubber sole on the top stair. He must have been walking along a dusty road and some of the dust clung to his shoes.' Tess grinned, rather pleased with herself, then her face sobered again. 'It's odd, though—nothing's missing and whoever it was has vanished again.'

'Shouldn't we ring the police?' Dottie asked anxiously.

'I'll ring Madame Beringer first—she may know if Hal asked the plumber or a builder to pop round to do some work. I wouldn't be surprised to find that that explains it—workmen tire so easily, he probably came over faint and had to lie down on my bed.'

Dottie laughed, walking into the kitchen to put down the shopping bags. Tess bent to pick up the bag Dottie had dropped earlier and at that second heard a scream from the kitchen.

'What is it?' Tess hurtled into the room and found Dottie staring into the garden.

'There he is!'

'My God,' Tess said, as she saw him a second later. 'I was right—he is six foot.' He had black hair, too, the light gleamed on it as he lounged in a chair on the patio as if he belonged there, his lean body completely relaxed. He was broad-shouldered and long-legged, casually dressed in an open-necked shirt and cream pants; he didn't look like a dangerous criminal but on the other hand he didn't look like a plumber, either.

'He's eating my muesli!' Dottie said with fury and tore out of the room with Tess on her heels, pausing to snatch up the gold-headed cane. Tess would have gone to ring the police before recklessly charging off to confront him but Dottie was always prone to plunging into situations without looking both ways first.

Dottie tore across the paving stones, her cork-heeled sandals clacking like a flock of woodpeckers, and the stranger swung round to stare at her, a spoonful of muesli paused in mid-air. Breathless, Dottie gasped out, 'Who are you? What are you doing here? How did you get into the villa?' And then, resentfully eying the muesli, added crossly: 'And you can put that spoon down—that's my muesli you've stolen!'

Tess almost cannoned into Dottie as she arrived and Dottie gave her an impatient look. 'Have you rung the police?' Her eyes urged Tess to reply in the affirmative and Tess promptly did, nodding.

'Yes, they'll be here any minute.' Dottie gave the stranger a triumphant stare.

'So you'd better be on your way fast, mister!' She waited for him to show signs of alarm and haste but he simply put the spoonful of muesli in his mouth and munched. Dottie looked crestfallen, bewildered. She turned to gaze appealingly at Tess who mouthed at her, 'French?' Dottie looked back at the stranger who had almost finished the muesli now and was happily ignoring them. '*Monsieur?*' Dottie said loudly and he looked up, stretching his long legs contentedly and smiling at her with lazy charm. He had a lean, tanned face, his cheekbones angular and his nose long with a hint of arrogance in the modelling of it. Expressionless, his face was austere, the stamp of authority on that firm mouth, that decisive chin. When he smiled, though, he looked very different, and Tess watched with irritation as he coolly assessed Dottie's curvy figure while Dottie, infuriatingly, went pink and lowered her eyes.

'*Monsieur, vous êtes* . . . what's the French for trespassing, Tess?' Dottie hissed.

'I'm not French,' the stranger drawled in a deep voice with the husky note of amusement in it, and Dottie's eyes opened wide.

'Oh—you look French,' she said and Tess scowled sideways at her—sometimes Dottie was almost simple-minded, why was she gazing at him like that?

'If you're English, why didn't you answer us just now?' she demanded and he gave her a shrug of amused mockery.

'I was eating. I don't like being interrupted in the middle of a meal.'

'Oh, come off it,' Tess exploded. 'You were giving yourself time to think up some excuse for being here, weren't you?'

'I don't need an excuse—I've rented the place for the next fortnight,' he lied calmly.

'Oh, no, you haven't,' Tess contradicted. 'My brother owns the villa and he would have told me if he had let it to anyone else. We're staying here and when the police arrive you can explain to them how you got into the villa and what you intended to do after you'd finished your so-called meal—got a van parked somewhere around, have you? Planned to load everything portable into it and make off without anyone being the wiser!'

He considered her drily, she saw the white flash of teeth against smooth tanned skin and felt a prickle of resentment of his good looks. Tess had good reason to distrust and dislike good-looking men; they were usually spoilt, vain, totally unreliable and sexual opportunists to whom fidelity was only a word. She was more than ready to believe that this man was no exception to that rule—he was far too attractive and too aware of it. Tess felt the slow speculation of his stare and disliked him even more—she knew what he was thinking as he looked from her to Dottie and smiled. Tess had been described as 'interesting' by one guy who tried hard to fall in love with her but never quite made it, but her face was too irregular for prettiness and her figure too slender for sex appeal.

Shifting his legs, the stranger pushed a hand into his trouser pocket and Tess stiffened, suddenly afraid he was going to produce a gun. Instead, he pulled out a key with a cardboard label on it, dangling it in front of her.

'I let myself in with the key I'd been given,' he murmured without visible signs of dismay.

'By whom?' Tess snapped, eyes narrowed.

'By the man who owns this villa,' he drawled, then looked into her sharp blues eyes with a mocking little smile. 'And I doubt very much if he is your brother unless you were a very late arrival in your parents' lives.'

Dottie settled with her chin on her hands, gazing from one to the other of them with bright-eyed fascination as though at a play.

Tess breathed carefully, counting to ten before she let her temper roar. She didn't like the way his grey eyes teased any more than she had liked the way they had run over her, absorbed every inch of her slight, briefly clad body and then decided she wasn't worth a second look.

'And what's the name of this man who gave you the key?' she insisted, wondering if her brother had left the villa in the hands of an agent locally who had let the place without informing him.

'Johnny Linden,' he said, watching her with a dry smile.

Dottie gasped and began to laugh. Tess slowly put down the gold-headed cane and almost fell into one of the other chairs.

'I see you know him,' said the intruder lazily.

'He's my father,' Tess said through clenched teeth. She might have known; Johnny had never bothered with ordinary conventions, it wouldn't enter his head to mention to anyone that he had cheerfully told a total stranger that he could borrow Hal's villa for a fortnight. He certainly couldn't have told Hal because Tess knew how scrupulous about details her brother was—he wouldn't have forgotten all about it if he had ever known in the first place.

'Your father?'

Tess didn't like the way he said it but she wasn't surprised by the disbelief in his face.

Anyone who had ever seen her father always looked at her like that when they first discovered whose daughter she was—with incredulity, as if she couldn't be telling the truth, with embarrassment because they were sorry for her, with secret amusement because she was a changeling, she didn't resemble her father at all. Johnny Linden had been one of the most beautiful men of his generation—much-photographed, much-painted by famous artists of his youth, he had been one of those faces which become the image of a whole period. Even today he could still turn heads and make women's eyes dream, although he was over fifty.

'That's right,' she said defiantly, her small chin lifted with belligerence. 'And he had no right to let the villa to you because he doesn't own it. My brother owns it and he has lent it to me for a fortnight, so I'm afraid you'll have to leave. I'm sorry if it's inconvenient,' she added, seeing his grey eyes harden and narrow to steel slits. 'But obviously there's been some mistake. I'm sure you'll be able to find somewhere else—a hotel or another villa.'

'I'm not going anywhere,' the stranger said in a cool, firm voice. 'I've paid two weeks' rent for this place and I'm staying.'

'Don't be ridiculous—you can't,' Tess spluttered, then added shrewdly, 'We got here first, you arrived while we were out shopping but we had already moved our cases into the villa. Where are yours?'

'In the boot of my car, at the garage, where I

had to leave it because something had gone wrong with the steering. They've promised to let me have it back as soon as they've fixed whatever's wrong, but that could take a couple of days, I gather, so I'm without transport for the moment.'

'Oh, you poor man!' Dottie said sympathetically. 'You are having a bad day, aren't you? First your car—and then this muddle over the villa! Isn't it always the same with holidays, haven't you noticed? Something always goes wrong no matter how carefully you've planned it. But don't worry, I'm sure we can sort something out. There are four bedrooms, after all.'

Tess seethed, not believing her ears. Dottie couldn't seriously be inviting this man to stay on at the villa with them?

'I'm Dorothy Wilmslow,' Dottie said, holding out her hand.

'Steve Houghton,' the stranger said, taking her hand and not giving it back for at least a minute while he smiled at her. 'I was about to point out that there was plenty of room and I'm really very respectable—Mr Linden will give me a reference, if you feel you need one.'

'Dottie,' Tess said in leashed fury, 'I'd like a word.' She walked away and Dottie followed after a slight hesitation. Out of earshot of Steve Houghton Tess turned on her friend, hissing. 'I don't want that guy lurking around for the next two weeks—he's not staying, whatever made you suggest that he could? We don't know anything about him, he could be a multiple murderer for all we know and he's certainly not my idea of a holiday companion. I'm going to tell him he has to go and you'd better back me up.'

'Oh, Tess,' protested Dottie, pleading in her face. 'You can't do that to the poor man . . .'

'Poor man?' Tess repeated. 'Poor man? Didn't the late, unlamented Howard teach you anything about men like that? One look at this guy and I could see he was pure poison, he probably breaks hearts the way other people eat peanuts—he grabs every girl he sees and gobbles her up. Is that what you want to be? Junk food for guys like him?'

Dottie gave her an unexpectedly shrewd look. 'You don't like him because he knows your father, you never like your father's friends.' She saw the angry flush rise in Tess's face and added quickly and soothingly, 'I understand how you must feel! It must be tough being the daughter of such a famous man—always in his shadow, being compared to him and always having people call you Johnny Linden's daughter as if you weren't anything but that. I've often thought I'd simply hate it.'

'You can't even begin to imagine,' Tess burst out hoarsely, then stopped dead, unable to say any more, not so much to protect herself as to protect her mother, who had never once, in Tess's hearing, said a word against Johnny or hinted at the pain and humiliation she must have had to suffer for years.

'I can,' Dottie blithely insisted in her innocence. 'Really, Tess, I realise it must have been a bore, but you can't turn Steve away simply because you're sick of being Johnny Linden's daughter! Your father's been paid two weeks' rent, remember. Steve has paid to stay here and he's driven all this way, only to have his car break down; he's stranded here and we can't make him leave. At least let him stay until his car has been fixed.'

Tess eyed her cynically. 'You fancy him,' she accused.

Dottie giggled and Tess couldn't help laughing with despairing amusement. 'You are a fool, Dottie,' she said.

'I know,' Dottie said. 'But he is rather gorgeous, don't you think?'

'A peacock,' Tess said drily. 'And don't you love the way he flaunts it?'

Dottie said with a self-deriding chuckle: 'Well, you know the saying—the hair of the dog?'

'How apt,' Tess said and got a hopeful look from her friend.

'He can stay then?'

'Can I stop you making an idiot of yourself? If you're determined on keeping him here, why should I stand in your way? Just don't ask me to sympathise when it's over and he has gone.'

'Maybe this time,' Dottie said yearningly and Tess shook her head with disbelieving pity.

'You are in a class of your own, Dorothy Wilmslow. You go back to square one with every new man—you don't learn a thing.'

'You're too cynical,' Dottie defended. 'That can be just as bad, you know.' She walked off back to where Steve Houghton lounged under the fluttering umbrella, watching them with narrowed, alert eyes. Tess heard Dottie talking, laughing, and felt the man throw a sideways look in her direction; she could guess what he was thinking—that he had won, the two of them had been a walk-over. Well, he was right where Dottie was concerned, but Tess was armoured against men like him. She hadn't grown up in Johnny Linden's shadow without learning the cruel side of beauty.

CHAPTER TWO

TESS put away all the food they had bought, then went upstairs to unpack her cases and put away her clothes, her face set in rigid lines as she moved slowly about the room. The very sound of Johnny's name still set her teeth on edge—she could feel her jaw aching with tension as she slid a pile of filmy underwear into a drawer. She rarely saw her father if she could avoid it, and when she did she had nothing to say to him. Her mother might be able to forgive and forget, but Tess had suffered agonies of embarrassment and misery because of her father's much publicised affairs. Her childhood had been ruined by the teasing of her friends, the curiosity of the adults around her, the awareness of her mother's silent unhappiness. The fact that her mother never mentioned the stories which appeared so often in gossip columns and women's magazines didn't lessen Tess's anger and resentment, it deepened them. Her mother's loyalty was a measure of her father's infidelity, made it clear how much her mother loved the man who was constantly seen with other women. Tess couldn't understand why her mother didn't divorce Johnny; she half despised her as she grew up, beginning to see her mother's silence as cowardice and a slavish inability to break free of a husband who didn't love her.

Once she had been driven to protest: 'Why don't you leave him? Get a divorce?' and her mother had looked at her with a calm sadness, smiling gently.

'I love him, Tess. You don't understand . . .'

'What is there to understand?' Tess had flared at once, her face flushed. At eighteen she had been quick to anger, hot-tempered and emotionally volatile, seeing everything in black and white, blind to the half-tones life more often showed instead.

'How can you put up with it?' she had said scornfully, staring at her mother with fierce eyes. 'Haven't you got any pride? I wouldn't stand for it, you can be sure of that—no man would ever treat me the way he treats you.' She had seen her mother pale and been stricken with remorse, biting her lower lip and muttering: 'Sorry, I didn't mean to upset you, but I don't *understand*,' and then her mother had smiled again, waveringly, and shaken her head at Tess.

'It isn't as important as you think,' she had said, unbelievably, and Tess had been speechless in bewilderment. She had known then, with dazed incredulity, that her mother was ready to put up with all Johnny's infidelities rather than lose him, and shock had silenced her. She never mentioned it to her mother again.

When she had finished her unpacking she looked at her watch—time for a swim before she made the supper. She bolted her door, stripped and put on one of the bikinis she had brought with her.

When she walked out into the sunshine she found Dottie and Steve Houghton still sitting at the table. They had been drinking some of the Perrier which Tess had put into the fridge; it looked very inviting with ice and a slice of lemon bobbing in it and Tess was irritated because she could see that Steve Houghton's presence was going to mean that Dottie was going to wait on him hand and foot, leaving Tess to her own company.

Dottie looked round, saying, 'Hey! That's a good idea, I'm going to change and have a swim—what about you, Steve?'

'My cases haven't been brought up from the garage yet,' he drawled, staring at Tess. 'They promised to bring them at around seven—it's nearly that now. You run and change, Dottie, and I'll join you in the pool later.'

'Okay,' Dottie said, disappearing into the villa.

Tess walked across the paved terrace and dived into the pool with more haste than grace because she found Steve Houghton's stare unnerving. The brief white bikini made her lack of curves too apparent; she had small, high breasts and narrow hips, a boyish figure she bitterly resented, especially when a man like that was watching her. She sensed a distinct mockery in his grey eyes and hoped he was going to follow Dottie into the villa, but when he got up he strolled over to the side of the pool and followed the rapid streak of her body through the blue water. Throwing him a furtive glance she saw that he had put on dark sunglasses which hid the expression of his eyes but didn't disguise the dry curve of his mouth. He was laughing at her and Tess put on speed as she passed him, deliberately splashing water upwards as her arms flailed the pool.

When she turned to come back he had gone and she slowed her pace just as Dottie appeared, generously filling a vivid red bikini even smaller than the one Tess wore.

'I look like a milk bottle,' she wailed as she lowered herself gingerly into the pool.

'I got a tan when I was here in the spring and it hasn't faded yet,' Tess said.

'The car from the garage has just delivered Steve's cases so he'll be joining us in a minute,' Dottie said as she swam off to the other end of the pool.

Tess grimaced, then did a few fast lengths of the pool before she climbed out, sleeking back her short, wet hair as she bent to pick up the short towelling robe she had flung on to the paved terrace.

Dottie's head bobbed up above the tiled edge of the pool. 'You aren't going in already?'

'I'm hungry, I'm going to start getting the supper,' Tess said evasively, and Dottie stared after her with obvious curiosity.

Tess met Steve Houghton coming out of the villa. Stripped, he was even sexier, and she gave him a defiant, reluctant smile, impatiently aware of the deep bronze of his hard, slim body, the smooth-skinned shoulders and long, muscled legs. He looked sensational, and he knew it; Tess wished she didn't know it, too.

He paused, lifting one dark brow into an arch of mockery. 'You didn't stay in long!'

She told him what she had told Dottie; the excuse didn't seem to ring any more true and he smiled disbelievingly at her.

'Dottie tells me the two of you run a boutique in Chelsea,' he murmured, lounging in front of her so that she couldn't get past him into the house.

'That's right,' she said shortly, then with a flare of irritation, 'Are you an actor, Mr Houghton?' How else could he have met her father? He was the same type.

'Steve,' he said softly, then said, 'You mean you've never heard of me?' as though he couldn't believe that.

Tess looked at him contemptuously; that had hit his vanity, had it? 'I'm afraid not,' she said with pleasure.

He stared down at her, reading the triumph in her angry dark-blue eyes, his face veiled and whatever thoughts he had kept well out of sight. Sunlight glinted on his thick black hair, giving it a sheen which emphasised the tan of his skin.

'Somehow, I get the impression you don't like actors much,' he said slowly.

'Percipient of you,' Tess snapped.

He laughed and she flushed. 'What long words you know,' he mocked and she felt childish immediately, which she knew he had intended, the silvery gleam of his eyes told her so. 'What's wrong with actors?' he enquired calmly, but there was more to the casual question than showed on the surface. Tess felt her nerves prickle and was at once wary.

'They're usually rather boring,' she shrugged, stepping sideways to escape. He blocked her, still smiling.

'I won't argue with that. I don't have your personal knowledge of actors off stage, but I'm ready to believe that they can be a bore.' He eyed her teasingly. 'And by the way—I'm a writer, not an actor.'

Tess frowned. 'What do you write?' His admission surprised her.

'Plays—I've written a couple.'

'Houghton,' she said slowly. 'Oh, yes, I remember—you wrote the last play my father did, didn't you? *Dumb Treason*—I saw it twice.' Somewhat reluctantly she admitted: 'It was very good.'

'How kind,' he said and laughed, as though her frowning reluctance amused him.

'I must get the supper,' Tess said through her teeth, scowling at him openly by now. He moved out of her way at last and she hurtled through the door into the silent villa in case he changed his mind and thought of something else to tease her with. She had been convinced he was an actor— he had all the narcissistic charm of her father, that smiling awareness of his own good looks and ability to make women go weak at the knees. Faced with his male beauty, the power and lithe grace of his tanned body, Tess had felt insignificant, diminished, bitterly conscious of her own lack of beauty. Something ached inside her as she changed and put on pink denim pants and a striped T-shirt; she felt an old grief again, a longing to look into the mirror one day and find herself utterly changed, given a new face and a more exciting body to go with it.

She heard voices and laughter from the pool while she was making the supper, the kitchen window open above her head. She viciously tore lettuce apart, sliced tomatoes and cucumbers, de-seeded peppers and crushed garlic while she decided that the second Steve Houghton's car had been fixed he must go. She wasn't playing gooseberry to him and Dottie, no matter how much Dottie complained. It might be helping Dottie get over her heartbreak but there was a limit to Tess's friendship and having Steve Houghton look her over in that mocking, dismissive way was more than flesh and blood could stand.

As a small child she had often run off to cry in her own room after her father's friends had stared down at her sulky little face and laughed, saying, 'She's *your* daughter? I'd never have guessed.'

'She takes after her mother,' Johnny had always said quickly, and it was true. Ellen did have the same slight build and blue eyes, the same dark hair which had turned a distinguished silvery shade when she was in her forties. Ellen wasn't beautiful, either; she was tranquil and quiet, her face had sensitivity and gentle intelligence but her mouth was too wide and she had a snub nose. People liked Ellen, she had a wide circle of friends and she was always busy because she couldn't bear to sit still doing nothing. She cooked and gardened and ran local committees, she sewed and embroidered and bottled fruit and made jam. While Johnny spun, glittering, across the London theatrical sky, Ellen was back at home in a small Sussex village in a very different world. Those two worlds didn't ever meet and Ellen almost never stepped from hers into Johnny's; she disliked the claustrophobic atmosphere of the theatre and preferred to stay where she was and have her husband occasionally visit her.

It was an odd idea of marriage, Tess thought, beginning to cook the veal escalopes. She leaned out of the window and yelled to Dottie. 'Supper in five minutes!' then jumped as a shape materialised in the doorway behind her. She spun, heart drumming. 'Oh, it's you,' she said shakily as she realised it was Steve Houghton. 'I thought you were still in the pool.'

'Dottie is,' he said, walking into the kitchen in cut-off jeans and a dark blue cotton sailor's jersey. 'Can I help?'

You could go away, thought Tess, staring at him. That would be a big help—I might begin to enjoy this holiday if you made yourself scarce. Her eyes might have said as much, but aloud she said politely, 'You could lay the table if you like—the dining area is in the hall.'

'Sure,' he said. 'Where do I find everything?'

'There's a sideboard in the hall beside the

dining table—everything you'll need is in that; table mats, glasses, cutlery.'

'It's very good of you to provide me with a meal,' he said, showing no sign of haste. 'Tomorrow you must let me take you and Dottie out to dinner somewhere special, and I'll pay for any more food we buy. I'm very sorry there's been this mix-up and as soon as I've got my car back and can shove off I'll go and look for other accommodation.'

Tess managed a polite smile. 'Okay, Mr Houghton.'

'Steve,' he corrected as he turned to go into the hall, throwing her a glance through those thick dark lashes which would have looked better on a girl.

She was just beginning to serve the meal when Dottie finally appeared; her damp hair tied up at the back of her head and a transparent flowered gauzy robe floating around her; she had tied it around her breasts, under her arms, with a careless panache which Tess couldn't have carried off.

Steve gave the outfit an appreciative smile, producing a bottle of local wine which, he said, the garage mechanic had brought up with his luggage.

'He says your hire car is ready for you tomorrow morning,' he told Tess, pouring white wine into her glass.

'Oh, great,' Dottie said. 'We'll be able to explore, won't we, Tess? Do you know this part of France well, Steve?'

Tess happened to be watching him help himself to salad—she saw the swift lowering of his lids, the sudden cool blankness of his face and knew he was somehow reluctant to answer, although she couldn't fathom why he should be wary of such an innocent question.

'I've been in this region before,' he admitted. 'Is this home-made mayonnaise?'

'No, shop bought, and very fattening,' Tess said, pouring her own vinegar and lemon dressing on to the salad.

He laughed incredulously, staring at her. 'You don't need to diet—you're skinny enough now.'

A little spot of red burnt in each cheek. Tess didn't look up, beginning to eat her supper. Dottie hurriedly leaned over and began to talk about the towns she wanted to visit and had never seen before.

While they were drinking their coffee Steve asked Tess casually if her family spent much of the year at the villa.

'We all come here—but it belongs to my brother and it's his family that uses it mostly.'

'What about your parents?'

'My mother comes occasionally. My father sometimes comes here between plays.'

'Alone?'

Tess laughed cynically. 'Johnny is never alone,' she said, then stiffened, realising she was breaking one of her own rules—she never discussed her father with anyone, she didn't know why she had just come close to it now. She must have drunk too much wine; it had gone to her head after the long day of travelling, followed by sun, swimming and nervous strain.

Dottie was sleepy, too. She was slumped over her coffee, her elbows on the table, yawning, oblivious of what was being said.

Steve Houghton poured himself another cup of coffee; his face was unreadable. He didn't seem to have noticed Tess's slip.

'I've never seen a picture of your mother in the newspapers—she keeps very much in the background, does she?' he asked casually.

'Yes,' Tess said shortly. 'I'll clear the table now, I think and get to bed—I'm sleepy and so is Dottie, by the look of her.'

'What?' Dottie blinked, yawning with small white teeth and pink gums on display.

'You look like a dormouse,' Steve said, laughing, and Dottie gave him a flattered smile.

'I'll do the washing up,' Steve said, rising, and Tess threw him a dry smile.

'Thanks.' She didn't try to argue him out of it. She helped him carry the plates and cutlery into the kitchen, then slipped away, leaving him to Dottie who wasn't apparently planning to abandon him just yet.

Tess undressed and got into bed, already half asleep, but before she drifted off into oblivion she reminded herself that Steve Houghton moved in the same world as her father and she mustn't ever again slip into discussing her parents with him. Gossip spread like wildfire; her loyalty to her mother outweighed any feelings she had about her father. It would hurt Ellen if she found out that Tess had even hinted at public criticism of her father. Tess had learnt to hold her tongue years ago and Steve Houghton certainly wasn't getting anything out of her.

She wasn't surprised next morning to find herself alone out on the patio eating a breakfast of orange juice, coffee and croissants. Dottie would probably sleep until quite late; on holiday she tended to indulge herself in all directions. Tess meant to walk down to the village garage to collect their car as soon as she had eaten. She could pick up some newly baked bread on the way back, they had everything else they needed.

She was just finishing her second cup of coffee when Steve Houghton appeared in jogging clothes, his black hair dishevelled and his face faintly flushed.

'Have you been for a run?' she asked, surprised.

He fell into the chair opposite, grinning. 'I always do two miles before breakfast.'

'How energetic of you.' Tess said derisively because she detected the crowing self-congratulation she found so maddening in her father. Johnny couldn't achieve anything without an audience to applaud and admire; perhaps that was why he was chronically unfaithful to her mother? He felt he had to have a constant change of audience, even in his love life.

Steve gave her a narrow-eyed stare. 'I wish I knew what was eating you,' he said. 'Are you always this acidic?'

'Always,' she assured him, getting up. 'Feel

free to make yourself some coffee—orange juice in the fridge, croissants in the larder.' Pausing she gave him a cool smile. 'I'm going down to the garage—I'll ask how much longer they're going to take with your car, shall I?'

'Do that,' he said tersely, knowing she wanted to get rid of him, and she walked away, satisfied with having made him frown. If he thought she was going to give at the knees just because he turned his mocking eyes in her direction, he could think again. She hadn't invited him to move into the villa—and it wasn't her fault if her father had told him he could rent it when the villa wasn't available.

As she walked along the sunlit lane she began to think hard—she was sure that Steve's play had been a smash hit, hadn't it run for nearly a year? He must be pretty well-off, he certainly dressed with style. Surely he could afford to stay at a good hotel? Why was he insisting on staying here? Was he merely careful with his money or had he some other motive?

Of course, it could simply be that having arrived and found two unattached girls at the villa he had thought he was on to a good thing. Dottie hadn't discouraged that idea, having taken one look at him she had welcomed him with open arms. It couldn't be shortage of money—Johnny was going to have to repay the rent he had paid and Steve Houghton could obviously pay the rates at one of the local hotels.

Tess told herself she was imagining things, but ever since last night she had had a distinct sense of uneasiness about Steve Houghton; sometimes when she looked at him before he had time to look away she had glimpsed a watchfulness in his eyes that she couldn't account for. Was he what he claimed to be? Maybe she ought to ring her father and check up on him—after all, they only had Steve's word for it that he was who he said he was!

She collected the hire car, picked up some crisp newly baked bread and drove back to the villa to find Dottie up and looking spectacular in vivid yellow shorts and matching top while Steve drank black coffee with her, an amused expression on his face. He had changed from his jogging outfit into pale grey denims with a black silk tunic top. He managed to make the casual clothes look the height of elegance and Tess felt dusty and very dull in her blue shorts and T-shirt.

'Hi!' Dottie said, waving. 'Get the car? What make is it?'

'A Renault,' Tess said, and gave Steve a bland look. 'Your car should be ready tomorrow morning, isn't that good news? You'll be able to move on.'

Dottie's face fell. 'Well, we'll think about that tomorrow. Guess what! Steve has offered to take us to lunch at the Eden-Roc! I've always dreamt of going there; it's supposed to be fabulous, Steve says the food is out of this world.'

'So are the prices,' Tess said drily, staring at him. So he frequented the Eden-Roc, did he? She had been there once or twice with her father and knew that lunch there would probably set him back as much as he had paid to rent the villa for a week. So if he could afford that, why didn't he move out and find somewhere else to spend his holiday? Was it Dottie's sexy figure that was keeping him?

She felt a dart of suspicion as she met his cool, grey eyes and saw the lids droop quickly to hide them from her. What was he up to? Why was he so set on staying here? He was watching her now, the silver of his eyes a wary slit he didn't want her to notice—she had felt last night that he watched her more than he watched Dottie and she had told herself she was imagining it. No man would look at her if Dottie was around, yet although, in typical male fashion, he enjoyed flirting with Dottie when the opportunity arose, Tess had several times caught him watching her out of the corner of his eye and each time he had quickly looked away. He was constantly aware of her—that much she was almost sure about. What baffled her was the reason for his interest. It wasn't sexual; he wasn't trying to attract her. He almost seemed to want to watch her when she wasn't aware of him, as if he was reluctant to let her see his interest.

Was it just her imagination? Or was he at the villa for a more sinister reason than she had supposed? Her father was very rich, it would be very easy to kidnap her from the villa and have her over the border into Italy from here in a few hours.

'Don't you think it's a wonderful idea, though?' Dottie asked, looking slightly puzzled and Tess pulled herself together.

'Yes, wonderful,' she said. 'But I'll have to change if I'm going to have lunch at the Eden-Roc—they wouldn't even let me in looking like this.'

As she walked into the villa she felt Steve staring after her and sensed that he was aware of some of the questions fizzing inside her head. In her room she looked at herself in the mirror, frowning. Kidnap? Could that be what was behind his determination to stay on here? Surely not—it was too far-fetched, she was letting her imagination run away with her. Wasn't she?

CHAPTER THREE

'PINCH me, I'm dreaming,' Dottie whispered, her face ecstatic, as she stared down through the pine trees to the blue sea.

The Eden-Roc hotel was a palatial little world of its own, isolated in wooded grounds which ran down to a private beach on the rocky coast of Cap d'Antibes. Guests in white were playing tennis not far away and they could hear the laughter and splashes of others diving into the hotel's pool. The decor was opulent, the guests visibly expensive, their manner as well as their clothes marking them out as people to whom money was no object. Dottie inhaled the ambience and glowed with delight.

'What will you have to drink?' Steve asked, his eyes amused as they met Tess's. He wasn't laughing at Dottie, yet his mouth had a lazy, indulgent curve to it as though her excitement did amuse him.

' A Martini,' Tess said and the waiter nodded. Tess watched him bend to hear Dottie's murmured order, she was too awed to be able to talk clearly. This place was a million light years from their tiny Chelsea boutique which was badly lit and noisy with pop music blaring through a loudspeaker. The shop had the atmosphere of a London disco, deliberately so—their customers were largely teenage girls. Dottie was in heaven, too excited to talk to Tess or Steve; too busy staring around her looking for famous faces among the other guests.

Tess caught the smile the waiter gave Steve Houghton as he walked away. He hadn't asked Steve what he wanted to drink, she realised, and she asked Steve, 'Come here often?' in mocking tones because she was certain that he did, and that the waiter didn't need to ask what Steve wanted to drink because he knew from long acquaintance.

Steve eyed her thoughtfully. 'I've been here a few times.'

'I thought you might have,' Tess said, her dark-blue stare telling him that he wasn't fooling her, she didn't know what he was up to but she didn't trust him an inch.

Steve deliberately let his gaze wander down over her and she seethed with fury at the way he did it. Dottie had dressed up for the occasion, wearing a clinging white silk dress clipped together over her breasts with a small gold butterfly—but Tess had dressed down, selecting a pleated cream blouse and neat blue skirt. She looked cool and English and faintly demure, but Steve's mocking eyes made her squirm.

'Look at that dress,' Dottie breathed, staring across the room at a woman in an elegant concoction of jersey silk. 'Paris, I bet,' Dottie envied. 'Don't you wish we sold clothes like that, Tess?'

'We do okay,' Tess said defiantly, less to

Dottie than to Steve who wasn't showing any interest in the woman or her dress, his gaze still fixed on Tess.

'Ever thought about going on the stage, yourself?' he asked as the waiter brought their drinks.

'No,' Tess said succinctly. It had been the last career she would have chosen; she wouldn't have followed her father anywhere, least of all into the theatre.

'You have an expressive face,' he drawled. 'I'd have thought you were a natural for an acting career. Your voice is unusual, too; good pitch.'

'Thank you,' she said with fierce restraint and he laughed.

'Don't you like being talked about? Unusual—most women love it.'

'I'm not most women!'

His eyes looked directly into her own and she felt a strange swimming sensation as though she had vertigo and the room was spinning around her.

'What have you got against the theatre?' he asked softly, holding her eyes, and Tess struggled to break free of that hypnotic gaze. She looked away, breathless, and picked up her drink; holding it made her feel less threatened, although why Steve Houghton should make her feel as though she was walking on the edge of a cliff she did not know.

'Well,' Dottie said cheerfully, suddenly homing in on their quiet conversation as her fascination with the rest of the people in the Eden-Roc bar died away a little. 'You know what Tess's father is like! I don't suppose she wants to follow in *his* footsteps.'

Tess glared at her, silently telling her to shut up, and Dottie went pink and apologetic.

'Don't you get on with your father?' Steve's voice was light but the pretence of casual enquiry didn't fool Tess.

She looked away without answering and saw the woman in the Paris dress coming towards them with her eyes fixed on Steve. 'I think someone has recognised you.' she said with faint malice and saw his dark head swing and a startled look in his eyes. Was she mistaken or was that annoyance in his face?

'Steve, honey, I thought it was you!' the new arrival purred and Steve rose. He kissed her, but Tess felt it was with reluctance on his part, although certainly not on hers. She smiled into his eyes as she went on talking.

'Have you been in France long? Why didn't you call me? Very wicked of you, being at the Cape but not giving me a call! I'd have given a party for you. Is Anna with you?'

'No,' Steve said coolly.

'Oh, really?' The blonde woman seemed interested, she smiled more widely. 'Don't tell me you aren't together any more? I had heard rumours but I didn't believe them. What happened?'

Steve shrugged, then said quickly: 'How's Jean-Marc? Still doing well with the boats? I haven't seen him for ages, give him my regards.

And the two little ones? They must have shot up now. Pierre must be all of eight, mustn't he?'

'Nine,' the blonde said. She was slim and deeply tanned, and obviously older than she managed to look. Her hair was dyed and her dark eyebrows made that obvious; there were laughter lines around her mouth. Dottie was watching avidly, on edge for Steve to introduce them, but Tess sat quietly, suspecting that that was the last thing he would do—although she couldn't say why she felt so certain of that.

'It was wonderful to see you, I'll give you a call soon,' Steve said and the blonde slid a sideways look at the other two girls, her eyes widening.

'Don't forget, then,' she said amiably, smiling at Steve a second later, then walked away back to her own party. Steve sat down and Dottie let out a disappointed sigh.

'She's ravishing,' she hinted to Steve. 'Is she an actress? Have you worked with her?'

'She's the wife of a friend of mine,' Steve said coolly. 'Shall we ask for the menu or do you want another drink?' He smiled quickly. 'Or both?'

He seemed to be in no hurry to choose from the various items on the menu and discussed the dishes with the head waiter who hovered over them, yet Tess caught Steve glancing at his watch several times before looking around the bar. She gave her own order crisply and at once Steve argued that she had made the wrong choice. 'If you're going to have the duck, you ought to start with their famous langoustine—the sauce they serve with them is delicious.'

'I'll just have melon, thanks,' Tess said deliberately, but Dottie eagerly said she would have the langoustine.

'What are they?' she asked happily, and looked thrilled to hear that they were a form of small lobster. While Steve was languidly discussing the wine list with the wine waiter Dottie whispered to Tess: 'Hey, remember the burger bar we had lunch at the day before we left? Talk about worlds apart. Isn't this gorgeous?'

'Good heavens,' Steve said in loud amazement, looking across the room. 'There's Franco Mersini!'

Dottie sat upright, her eyes flying in search of the man whose name was vaguely familiar. Tess frowned, seeing a slimly built young man, in a white suit with a powder blue tie and dark blue shirt, looking around the bar in obvious search of someone.

'It *is* him!' Dottie breathed.

'Who?' Tess asked, alert with suspicion as Steve got up and waved.

'Franco Mersini—the pop star, well, Italian pop star—he doesn't make the top twenty in England but I saw him on TV in the Eurovision Song Contest. You remember, he sang that terrific ballad. Oh, he's coming over. He's even better looking in real life, on TV he looked rather yellow—isn't he brown? But then Italians are, aren't they? Lucky things, all that sun every day.' Dottie looked at Steve with enormous eyes. 'You know him?'

Steve was standing up. Oh, he knows him

all right! thought Tess as Steve said: 'Ciao, Franco!' and the newcomer answered with a rapid flow of Italian which Tess didn't understand although she was sure it was apologetic. Steve shrugged, clapped him on the shoulder and indicated the fourth chair at their table.

'You don't mind if Franco joins us, do you?' he asked the two girls, but he was looking at Dottie and she was sparkling excitedly, even if Tess was neutral.

'I should say not!' She wasn't one to waste time in delaying games; she looked at Franco's rather pretty face with open admiration. He was famous and Dottie respected fame; you could see that Franco's status was a halo round his head as far as she was concerned. Dottie wasn't a hypocrite or a snob, but she was genuinely excited by handsome men, especially when they turned out to be famous too.

Steve introduced them, the waiter came over and Franco ordered a vodka and tomato juice. He had the dark hair and eyes you would expect, the carefully tanned skin, the easy charm of someone used to talking to strangers and persuading them to like him.

'Are you staying here?' Dottie asked him, awed, and he shrugged modestly.

'It's a great hotel, isn't it?' He was looking across the table at Steve whose features were impassive, but Tess distinctly saw a flash of warning in Steve's eyes and at once Franco plunged into a description of the horrors of traffic along the Cote d'Azur. 'At least you can forget about that when you're in the Eden-Roc's grounds—they have so much room.' Tess watched Steve out of the corner of her eye. There was nothing haphazard about Franco's appearance, she suspected Steve had asked him to join them, perhaps he had phoned him when he had been jogging that morning. That explained why Steve hadn't hurried over ordering lunch. But why hadn't he told them that he'd asked someone to join them?

'I saw you in the Eurovision Song contest, you were terrific,' Dottie told Franco who looked modest again—he did that very well, he had a special smile which went with the little shrug.

Dottie had touched on Franco's favourite topic—himself. He turned in his chair and smilingly pursued the subject, encouraged by Dottie's breathless questions about his career, his background, his friends, his music. Tess glared at Steve through her lashes, wondering how he felt about Franco making a big play for Dottie when Steve had obviously invited him along to keep Tess occupied. If Steve didn't like it, he wasn't showing the fact.

'How long have you been running your boutique?' he asked her as though he was really interested and while she answered he watched her, sipping his drink slowly. It was a fairly safe subject, Tess suspected he couldn't be as interested as he pretended but she talked about the shop for a while because it avoided awkward silences.

'Did your father help with the finances?' he asked as she paused and Tess stiffened.

'No, I had a legacy from my grandfather—my mother's father. It was very useful but I missed him, he was a darling old man, we used to call him Dandy because he loved wearing smart clothes even when he was eighty.' She stopped abruptly, sensing Steve's real interest now. Why was he so curious about her and her family? He was always asking questions about them. She gave him an edgy smile.

'Who's Anna?' she asked because why should he always ask but never tell?

She saw the muscles of his face tighten, he made a big thing out of picking up his glass and swallowing the last of his drink. 'An old friend,' he said when he had had time to think.

'Old flame, you mean, of course,' Tess said sarcastically and he gave her a narrow look, but at that moment they were told that their table was ready. Tess hung back as she stood up, expecting Steve to take this opportunity of pairing up with Dottie, but Franco and Dottie walked off, still talking, and Steve gave Tess a mocking smile as he waved her forward. She was puzzled, frowning at him. What game was he playing? Why was he deliberately separating her from Dottie, getting her to himself?

'You've got quite a complex, haven't you?' Steve watched her intently, as if trying to work her out and she reacted to this speculation with immediate wariness, looking away so that all he could see was the edge of her small, mutinous

face; the defiant chin and set lips, the sleek cap of
black hair outlining her features. Her head only
came to his shoulder, she found his height
infuriating; just as she was irritated by his
spectacular good looks. He must always have seen
the world from a very different angle from her
own—attractive people do, they are used to
meeting smiles and getting attention. Tess had
had to fight to get her own strip of personal
territory, her own sense of herself. When you
have to fight like that you need pugnacity, you
have to use all your natural aggression and
tenacity to grab and hold on to what you want.

'What's your brother like?' Steve asked her
during lunch and it was only one of a series of
probing questions she had managed to evade.

'To look at? Oh, he's broad and has brown
hair, he's five foot ten and pretty solidly built and
he's got hazel eyes.' She was deliberately making
the answer simple.

'There are only the two of you, aren't there?
Your father doesn't have any other children?'

It was an odd question, phrased like that, and
Tess shot him a curious, glinting look.

'Yes, there are only the two of us.'

'Your brother didn't go into the theatre either?'

'No, he's in advertising—he's done very well,
too. He's very successful.' She turned to face him
belligerently. 'Anything else you want to know
about my family?'

The brusque question didn't throw him—he
smiled blandly. 'Your family fascinates me—
what's it like to have such a famous father?'

'Don't ask unanswerable questions,' she muttered, drinking the cool dry wine that had been served with her duck. She hadn't seen the wine list and didn't know how much it had cost but she knew enough about wines to guess that it had been very expensive. She had had three glasses of it so far, her head was faintly cloudy, she should stop now before she lost all her inhibitions and said something outrageous to Steve Houghton. She was finding it hard to keep her cool now; he kept pushing her to tell him things she had never told anyone. She wished she knew why he wanted to know so much about her family.

'Did you wish you had a very different father?' he insisted, summoning the wine waiter with a casual lift of his hand.

'No, thank you,' Tess said hurriedly, covering her glass with her hand. 'I've had enough.'

'Nonsense,' Steve said, taking her hand away and holding it firmly while the waiter refilled her glass.

Tess turned in fury, her blue eyes spitting fire. 'I didn't want any more wine.' He didn't relinquish her hand, his fingers had twined around hers, she felt their tips brushing the back of her hand. He leaned towards her, smiling.

'Don't,' she said huskily because for a split second she had thought he was going to kiss her, and she watched his black brows arch in amusement.

'Don't what?' he mocked.

Tess looked confused. She pulled her hand free

and automatically picked up her glass to drink some more wine. That was a mistake, she knew it, even as she drained her glass. Her head was so light it felt as if she was floating high above them all; she needed something to anchor her down and gripped the edge of the table.

Dottie was giggling a good deal; she had been monopolised over lunch by Franco, and their lively chatter had been an odd counterpoint to the question and answer session going on between Steve and Tess. From time to time Tess had tuned in to their conversation, they had talked of the South of France, pop music, film stars, sailing and anything else that floated through Dottie's head.

As they drank their coffee, Dottie leaned over excitedly. 'Tess, Franco owns a power boat—he's going to take us out in it after lunch! Won't that be terrific?'

Tess swallowed in dismay. 'Oh, I'm sorry, I couldn't face sailing now,' she said. 'I get sea sick if I sail after a heavy meal.' She had found that out years ago and shuddered at the very idea of bumping along from wave to wave, her stomach churning.

Dottie's face fell. 'Oh, don't be a spoilsport, Tess!'

'You will not be seasick in my boat, she is as smooth as silk,' Franco insisted.

'I'm dying to go,' Dottie said in a disappointed voice. 'Franco was going to sail along the coast as far as Menton—we'd be able to see the Italian coast and I've never been to Italy.'

Tess suddenly felt cold, she sensed Steve's eyes watching her and glanced at him quickly. He looked away, his expression casual.

'It's a wonderful day for sailing; the sea is as calm as a duck pond,' he said persuasively. 'You couldn't be seasick on a day like this, could she, Franco?'

'Impossible,' Franco insisted. 'We will sail slowly, if you are afraid—I won't race.' He smiled coaxingly but Tess caught the quick look he and Steve exchanged, saw Steve's clear-edged profile tense.

They wanted her to sail along the coast in Franco's boat very badly—why? What had Dottie said about going to Menton, seeing the Italian coast? Tess found it hard to think, she was still bemused by the wine, but instinct warned her against agreeing. Steve Houghton wasn't getting her to Italy, if that was his plan he could forget it.

'Sorry, I want to sleep this lunch off,' she said, yawning and covering her mouth with one hand. 'I'm so sleepy, I must go back to the villa.'

'I can't go alone,' Dottie pleaded, eyeing her with reproach.

'You don't trust me?' Franco asked, pretending to be hurt, and Dottie looked at him anxiously, shaking her head at once.

'Don't be silly—it isn't that, but we only have one car and if Tess goes back to the villa, I'll have to go with her.'

'I take you for a sail and then I drive you back

to the villa,' Franco said cheerfully. 'Okay? Then Steve and Tess can do as they wish—we don't need them.' He grinned across the table at Steve. 'That's settled, yes?'

'Yes,' Steve said and Tess frowned, caught unawares. She opened her mouth to protest, say: hey, hang on! That wasn't what she had intended—she didn't want to find herself alone in the villa with Steve Houghton. She had simply wanted to make sure he didn't lure her on to a boat headed for Italy—she had been so sure that that was his plan but now she was confused. Was it another plan altogether that he and Franco had cooked up beforehand?

'Okay, we go now, pity to waste this perfect weather,' Franco said, getting up. 'See you later, Steve, have fun.'

'Bye, Tess—have a nice sleep,' Dottie said, vanishing while Tess was still too bemused to work out what she ought to do.

'Dottie!' she called, turning in her chair as she made up her mind, but her hand caught her wine glass as she swung round and she gasped in dismay as the contents spilled across the table. 'Oh, sorry,' she groaned, watching the waiter diving to right the glass and mop up the wine before it soaked into the damask cloth. 'Sorry,' she said in a slurred voice to Steve, her face very pink, then looked round again for Dottie, but Dottie had gone. 'Oh, damn,' Tess said to herself and Steve softly asked if anything was wrong.

'Feeling under the weather? I'll get you back to

the villa and bed,' he said, and Tess felt hot colour rush to her face as she took that promise in—what did he mean by *that*?

He paid the bill and guided her out of the hotel into her car; she gave a faint protest as she found herself in the passenger seat and Steve told her that she was in no state to drive. He seemed extraordinarily clear-headed and she lay back in the seat, trying to remember if he had drunk much wine, she hadn't noticed at the time but now she came to think about it he had been far more interested in keeping her glass full than worrying about his own.

She closed her eyes to think; it was very hot and the wine made her head heavy, her thoughts confused. Cool air rushed over her face as the car raced away from Cap d'Antibes towards Vence; it was a long drive and should give her time to think about what Steve Houghton was planning and why, but somehow Tess couldn't concentrate. She looked through her lashes at Steve, he was driving in an abstracted way, staring straight ahead, one long-fingered hand resting on the wheel, the other moving down to the gears. She felt it brush her leg and Steve turned to look at her. Tess pretended to be asleep; her pulses were beating a wild tattoo along her throat, she hoped he couldn't glimpse the agitation she was trying to hide. She had to keep a cool head, but when she had no real idea what was going on that wasn't so easy.

She didn't have to pretend to be asleep for long; she gradually eased into real sleep as they approached Grasse. The next she knew was when an arm slid between her and the warm fabric of the seat. She stirred, opening sleepy eyes, and found Steve's face an inch away. That was when she woke up and realised that he was lifting her bodily out of the car. Her flush intensified and she hastily muttered, 'I'm awake, I'll walk.'

They were parked outside the villa, she caught the scuttle of a small green lizard behind the swag of wisteria.

'As you like,' Steve said, putting her down on the paved terrace. She stumbled and righted herself, walked unsteadily to the front door and unlocked it. The cool, shadowy hall was delicious, she stood in it with eyes half-closed, trying to wake herself up fully, to remember what had been worrying her when they left the hotel. Dottie had gone off with Franco, she was alone with Steve. That was quite worrying enough for the moment. She looked round for him and there he was; sunlight glinting on his thick black hair. Her stomach lurched. My God, he's so good-looking, she thought drowningly, staring at the smooth tan of his skin, those brilliant grey eyes, that hard, warm mouth.

'Can you make it upstairs or shall I carry you?' he asked, and she had a reckless impulse to sway into his arms.

'I'm fine,' she said, nevertheless, taking a jerky step towards the stairs.

'Careful,' he said. 'Remember, there aren't any banisters.'

She was remembering it now, groping for the

wall for a hand-hold. Steve was right behind her, she felt his hand on her waist, steadying her, then he suddenly turned her towards him and as she gasped, swaying, he propelled her over his shoulder like a sack of potatoes and carried her up to her room.

A moment later she slithered on to the bed and lay there, heart thudding, eyes closed. 'I feel . . .' she began but the words faded away as Steve sat down next to her. 'What are you doing?' she managed as she felt his hand touching her.

'Undoing your blouse,' he said coolly, the buttons sliding out of their holes as if he undressed women all the time; and no doubt he did, she thought, pushing his hand away.

'You got me drunk,' she accused, because she was certain he had done it deliberately.

He was unzipping her skirt now and she beat his hand away from her waist, too. 'Stop that.'

'You don't want to sleep in your clothes, do you? You'll ruin them.'

It sounded reasonable enough; Tess frowned, opening her eyes and saw him, leaning over her, with a stab of attraction she didn't want to feel. He looked down into her eyes, his fingers busy again, she felt her skirt go and gave a faint moan of protest without looking away from those silvery eyes with their great black glowing pupils.

'What are you after?' she demanded huskily. He had some sort of conspiracy in mind; she might have found herself in Italy if she had agreed to go with Franco on that boat. What ransom would they have asked for? Would

Johnny have paid it? Idly, she wondered how much she was worth—to her father, to anyone?

'Is that a serious question?' Steve enquired, his mouth mocking.

'I'm on to you,' Tess told him. 'I know what you're plotting and you're wasting your time— Johnny wouldn't pay a bent farthing to get me back. He probably wouldn't even know who you were talking about when you told him you'd got me.'

Steve watched her intently, his smile no longer in evidence. 'Ransom?' he asked slowly, but although he was serious now his hands were still active and she struggled crossly as he removed her undone blouse.

'Don't pretend not to know what I'm talking about! You haven't fooled me, but you're fooling yourself if you think my father would pay to get me back.'

'You don't like your father much, do you?' he asked softly.

'You're pretty obvious, you know,' Tess muttered, wishing he wouldn't look at her because she hardly had a thing on now. She tried to grab the quilt to wrap herself up but as she leaned over, propped on one elbow, the ribbon strap of her slip slid down her arm and Steve put out a hand to pull it up again, his fingers cool on her bare shoulder. The touch of his hand did some drastic things to her heartbeat so she burst into stammered rage. 'Having Franco turn up like that at lunch—and then it turns out he's got a boat and he wants to take us to Menton—just across the border from Italy. Really! Hardly subtle, is it?'

'Your father wouldn't care if someone kidnapped you?'

'My father only cares about one person in this world.'

'You hate him, don't you?'

Tess looked confused; how had the conversation taken this turn again? Steve hadn't denied her accusations, he had simply swung the conversation back into a course which was becoming far too familiar. He was persistent, maddening as a gadfly, she shook her head as though to drive him away, and then realised that his hand was still smoothing her shoulder-blade. She looked down at it, squinting along her nose.

'Stop that.'

He smiled mockingly, sliding his hand downwards, it touched her breast and she took a deep, shaken breath, staring into his watchful eyes.

'You're not making love to me, so you can get your hands off me,' she said thickly, wagging a finger in front of his nose. 'You're not making love to me!' she repeated.

His head shot forward, he bit her finger and she gave a yelp. 'Don't put ideas in my head that weren't there,' Steve advised softly.

'No?' Tess felt a strange sinking in her insides. Hadn't he been thinking of it? She had—ever since he put her on the bed she had been waiting with fast-beating heart and a dry-mouthed tension for Steve to kiss her, she was longing to find out what it felt like to have his mouth touch hers. It wouldn't be like every other kiss she had ever had, she was sure of that. Who knew what might happen? The earth might shake, the world might come to an end, she would hear harps and see rainbows.

'If you insist, though,' Steve murmured, bending, and she could have pushed him away, she could have slapped his face or told him she'd rather die than let him kiss her. She could have. But she didn't. She put her arms round his neck and closed her eyes and his mouth was warm, teasing; it mocked and played with her, lifting and coming back in tiny butterfly kisses that drove her crazy so that she put a hand on the nape of his neck and pulled his head down to take his mouth with feverish need. She felt his arms encircle her, one on her back and the other moving on her hair, and Steve kissed her back with a passion that was slow to take fire but when it did made her whole body burn; she clasped his neck and her other hand felt its way, as if she were blind, over his warm body.

Without taking his mouth from hers, he pushed her slowly back on to the pillow and Tess trembled, moaning, feeling his hand exploring; the flesh he touched was so sensitive that she gasped—she had never been so intensely aware of her body before, the stroke of his fingers on her bare skin made her temperature climb.

Steve moved his lips from her mouth along her cheek, and then, his face against hers, whispered into her ear. 'I haven't many scruples, but seducing intoxicated women is one game I don't play. You don't know what you're doing, do you?'

Yes, of course I do—don't stop, Tess almost protested, her hand against the hard-beating vein in his throat which told her he was as aroused as she was, but some submerged instinct of self-preservation kept her silent, and Steve sat up, leaving her cold and aching with frustration.

'You'd better sleep it off,' he said, avoiding her eyes. He pulled a quilt over her and quietly left the room and Tess groaned, biting her lower lip. She wanted him, she closed her eyes and thought about the way his hand had softly cupped her breast, the repeated drug of his kisses which had incited rather than cured her fever. Heat burned between her thighs, her forehead was damp with sweat. She had never really understood why women did crazy things for men who treated them badly—she had never understood her mother's silent devotion to her father. Desire had always been a word and nothing more—but now she knew what that word meant and she twisted and turned on the bed in unsated craving for the new sensation she had only just discovered.

CHAPTER FOUR

THE moon woke Tess up; the white shimmer of moonlight soaking through her lids and reaching into her dreams. She tossed restlessly, yawned, sat up and felt her head thump heavily. 'Oh,' she winced, a hand to her forehead, for a second quite disorientated. 'I feel awful,' she told the moon which was shining directly into her window. Why weren't her shutters closed? She frowned, and then she remembered and consternation filled her face.

She almost fell out of bed and stared with horror at her reflection. What did she look like? A rumpled slip, a bra and panties—she looked dishevelled. She thought of another word for it but clamped her mouth shut on that and picked up her robe to go and have a shower to wake herself up.

All the way to the bathroom she kept remembering and flinching. What had she said to him? Oh, no! Oh, no, she thought. What had she done? 'Oh, no,' she moaned, turning the shower on and getting under it, masochistically letting the water run ice-cold and gritting her teeth at the sting of the needles of water.

How was she going to face him again? She'd have to leave, pack now and get out of the villa before he woke up. She got out of the shower, dried herself with angry punishing fingers and dressed in a workmanlike pair of denim pants and a blue and white striped top, then opened her door to listen—the house was silent. She had to think and she needed black coffee—strong, black coffee. So she stole down the stairs, her rubber-soled plimsolls making no sound on the stone, and went into the kitchen, only to stop short in shock as she saw the light on. For a second she dithered like a fool, but it wasn't Steve—it was Dottie, sitting at the table with her elbows propped on it, drinking coffee and yawning.

'Hi,' she said cheerfully and Tess shut the door behind her and looked at Dottie in impatient disbelief.

'It's four o'clock in the morning. What have you been up to all night?'

'Franco took me to Monte—we had supper and went to the casino. I couldn't leave while I was winning, could I? Look!' She pulled franc notes out of her purse and showered them on the table, giggling. 'Two thousand francs! That's about two hundred pounds. Isn't it wonderful?'

'You idiot! You can't afford to gamble! What if you'd lost?' Tess sat down and poured herself a cup of coffee; it was still quite hot and she wondered if it had been the moonlight or the sound of Dottie coming home that had woken her up.

'Party-pooper!'

'You're drunk!'

'I am not so,' Dottie said with dignity, swaying from side to side like an elephant, her head at an angle. 'We had to celebrate, didn't we? My first visit to Monte Carlo, my first visit to a casino and I broke the bank.'

'They won't even miss two thousand francs,' Tess said drily. 'Aren't you tired?'

Dottie leaned over to hiss at her. 'Stop raining on my parade. I had the night of my life—we sailed and we drove in the most beautiful car I've ever seen in my life and we had champagne and caviar and we gambled and I won and you are not being a little black rain cloud in my life so go and drizzle somewhere else.' She got up with dignity, somewhat spoiling this by lurching as she tripped over something on the floor which, when she peered angrily at it, did not seem to be visible.

She opened the kitchen door, hanging on to the handle. 'Good,' she said looking back at Tess and mouthing the word with slowed-down emphasis. 'Night.'

Tess laughed. 'Idiot.' Dottie wiggled her fingers and winked.

The door shut and opened again. Dottie stumbled in, grabbed up her franc notes and stuffed them back into her purse, then left again. Tess cleared the coffee things from the table, frowning. Dottie fell from one man problem to another. She always seemed to bounce in between, it was true. Her tragedies only had one act, but Tess recognised the symptoms now. If Franco stayed around, Dottie was going to be crazy about him, and as Tess was certain that Franco's arrival on the scene had been stage-managed by Steve she suspected that Franco would be whisked off stage quite soon.

She turned out the light as the moon sank and the sky was filled with that cool, colourless light which comes before the sunrise. The birds were restive; excitedly telling each other that the day was beginning, fluttering and flying among the cypresses and through the dancing silver olive leaves.

Tess went out into the garden and wandered along the paved paths, her face angrily confused. She couldn't leave without taking Dottie and Dottie was in no state to travel, but how on earth was she to look Steve Houghton in the eye?

Tess stopped dead under a cypress and watched the warm rose of the rising sun fill the dead grey sky. Why should *she* run away? She wasn't the intruder at the villa—Steve was! Steve was the one who should go and when she saw him she had to make that crystal clear. If he argued she would have to ring her father and get him to tell Steve . . . Tess's eyes widened. She must ring her father and find out everything she could about Steve Houghton. They only had his word for it that he had rented the villa from Johnny. In fact, now she was beginning to think calmly she realised that they only had his word for it that he was the Steve Houghton who had written Johnny's last play. He hadn't shown them his passport or a letter of authorisation from Johnny, he hadn't given them any proof that he was rightfully at the villa. He had a key—but, now that she came to think about it, wasn't there a key hidden in the garden hut in case of emergencies? She quickened her step and skirted the pool, went into the wooden hut in which the gardener kept his tools and equipment.

Frowning, she tried to remember where Hal put the key. Under a flowerpot? She lifted a few without finding anything, then her eye fell on a box marked Nails and she gave a triumphant whoop. That was where Hal kept the key. She opened the box hurriedly.

It was empty. She stared into it, biting her lip. That didn't prove that Steve had taken the key, of course. Hal might have forgotten to put it back. The gardener might have taken it. No, the only sure way of finding out was to ring her father. She looked at her watch. It was gone five now and Johnny would certainly be fast asleep until at least eleven o'clock. But he usually switched his 'phone on to the answering service at night, she remembered. She could leave a message and get him to send her a telegram. That might be wisest, anyway, because her father was more often out than in, and she could ring for days without managing to get hold of him in person.

She opened the gate before she got into the car and coasted silently down the drive without needing to turn on the engine because there was a steep incline from the side of the house to the road. As she swung out of the gates the engine flared into life and she looked into her wing mirror, watching the villa—would Steve hear the car?

She drove through the empty, silent lanes to the nearest public telephone box and parked. As she had expected, Johnny's answering machine was what she got and Tess dictated a message. She only just had enough change to make the call.

She didn't feel like going back to the villa; she was wide awake now and didn't want to see Steve too soon. She had to whip up her courage first. She drove around for a while, then stopped to buy hot bread and rolls from a village bakery where the assistants stared at her in amazement, not expecting customers so early or at least not strangers. A workman came in after her to buy himself rolls for his breakfast and as she left she saw a woman running across the village street in slippers and apron to get the hot croissants for the family. The village was stirring; she heard a dog barking and children shouting, '*Maman, du chocolat!*'

She drove back to the villa and as she parked beside the house saw Steve looming in the doorway, his hands on his hips and a frown on his forehead. He was dressed; in jeans and a white cotton sweater. He looked very awake, not to say dangerously vital.

'Where have you been?' he demanded, coming out to meet her, scowling.

'Buying the rolls for breakfast!' Tess was too alarmed by the implicit threat of his manner to remember her reasons for not wanting to see him.

'For over two hours?' he said through his teeth. 'Where did you go to get them? Paris?'

'Keep your voice down! Dottie's asleep upstairs,'

Tess hissed, then asked crossly, 'How do you know how long I've been gone?' She was clutching the bag of rolls and croissants and the two sticks of bread and the smell of the hot bread made her aware of being very hungry. 'And what's it to you anyway?' she added defiantly, walking past him into the villa. She could smell coffee and she headed for the kitchen without a backward glance, although very conscious that Steve was right behind her.

She dumped the bread on the kitchen table and poured herself a cup of coffee. This one tasted better than the cup she had drunk several hours ago—Steve made good coffee and Tess felt very healthy after her drive in the morning air.

'Sit down,' Steve said. 'I want to talk to you.'

Tess grabbed a croissant and a roll, put them on a plate and went to the fridge to get herself some orange juice. She ignored Steve. She had remembered last night again and she didn't want to meet his eyes or let him say anything, she had a feeling she wouldn't like whatever he planned to say.

'Did you hear what I said?' he asked, tight-lipped with fury.

'I'm not deaf and you're shouting,' Tess said, getting a small tray from the larder and piling her breakfast on to it.

'Where do you think you're going with that?' Steve stepped sideways and seized the other side of the tray as she headed for the door with it.

Tess glared at him across the tray, but that was a mistake because the flash of his silvery eyes made her throat close in alarm and she felt hot colour flowing up her face.

Steve took advantage of her momentary confusion to pull the tray out of her hands and push it back on to the table. Before Tess had pulled herself together he had deposited her on a chair by the simple expedient of taking hold of her shoulders and forcing her down backwards.

'Get your hands off me!' Tess reacted too slowly and when she tried to get up again Steve's long-fingered hands held her down, his body blocking her escape anyway.

'Now tell me where you've been since you drove out of the gates at five o'clock this morning?' he said, his mouth hard with the triumph of having made her do as he wished. Tess saw that satisfied expression and stiffened in outrage.

'You big bully!' she said with scathing contempt, and a slow dark red colour seeped into his face. 'What are you afraid of? That I might have gone to the police and told them about you?'

His lip curled back and she saw his clenched white teeth—he unclenched them with a visible effort and said in a voice he tried to control: '*That's* what I want to talk to you about—all that crazy nonsense about kidnapping and ransoms. What on earth put that idea into your head? Do I look like a Mafia boss?'

Tess surveyed him coolly, as though considering the question. 'Yes,' she decided. 'Yes, that's what you look like.'

Steve's hands tightened on her shoulder and he

shook her. 'I don't think this is funny,' he said and she wondered how he knew she was laughing because she had kept a very straight face. Although Steve was alarming in this menacing mood, she felt a relief that was almost euphoric because she found him far less worrying when he was angry than he had been last night when he kissed her. Aggression was a safer emotion than that piercing sexual attraction which had made her head swim and incited her to behave in a way she couldn't believe now that she remembered it in broad daylight when she was stone cold sober. That was it, though, wasn't it? She had been drunk. That was a comforting thought. She'd drunk too much wine and the moon had been too bright—excuses, excuses, she told herself angrily.

'You have an inventive imagination!' Steve told her. 'Franco's a very rich guy—he's sold millions of records, he's a big name in his world. What on earth makes you think that he'd be involved in anything like kidnapping?' He shrugged, his mouth fierce. 'We'll leave me out of it for the moment although I'm not exactly on the verge of bankruptcy either.'

'How can we leave you out of it?' Tess asked sweetly. 'You were the one who arranged to have Franco turn up at the Eden-Roc—and don't tell me he was there by accident because I just don't believe that. You stage-managed that for some reason of your own. I'm just guessing what that might be.'

He looked at her oddly through his black lashes

and her pulses beat frantically, although she ordered herself not to be susceptible to those intimate glances he used instead of plain words. He's manipulating you, she told herself, but she wasn't listening to common sense today. She was too busy watching the smooth brown of his throat, the hard angles of jaw and cheekbone, the almost sculptured lids half-covering his eyes. She knew she was a fool—Steve was putting on a show and she was a captive audience, she ought to walk out of the theatre but she couldn't stop looking.

'Okay, I rang Franco and asked him to join us at the Eden-Roc,' he admitted. 'Another guy seemed a good idea.'

'You can't cope with more than one woman at a time?' mocked Tess.

He gave her a glance which made her nerves leap—he hadn't liked that remark. 'Maybe I didn't want to,' he drawled and she laughed shortly.

'You asked Franco along for me, I suppose, but he preferred Dottie.'

'Is that what you want me to say? You know it isn't true.'

She felt heat prickling the back of her neck and looked down. 'Don't try to kid me that . . .' she broke off because she couldn't say what she wanted to say, it was too humiliating. Steve couldn't have wanted to be alone with *her*.

'I wanted to get to know you better without Dottie chattering in my other ear,' Steve said drily. 'She's a very pretty girl but she giggles too much and her brand of conversation tends to be flip repartee.'

'You seemed happy enough flirting with her when you first arrived.'

'She's a nice girl, very friendly—which is more than I can say about you.'

'But you wanted to see if you could make me friendlier,' Tess resented. Was that why he had made a pass at her yesterday? Was he the sort of man who hates to fail with any woman and will go all out to change indifference into doglike devotion, even when he isn't seriously interested in the woman in question?

Steve breathed roughly, a white line around his mouth. 'I'm rapidly losing my temper with you. Why are you determined to put the worst construction on everything I do or say?'

'I'm merely curious about your motives for being so interested in me!'

He eyed her, his mouth relaxing in a strangely wry smile and his brows arching quizzically. 'It couldn't possibly be simple biology?' he drawled and she went pink which only made him laugh aloud. 'Or are you going to pretend you've forgotten last night?' he murmured in a lowered tone as though they were conspirators in a house over-run by spies, and the next second he had lifted Tess out of the chair just as she gave a squawk of protest.

'No, I . . .' The words were stifled by the abrupt, sensual possession of his lips and she grasped his shoulders to thrust him away a second too late; his hand was on her back, forcing

her towards him and Tess weakly yielded to that
kiss for a moment, her eyes closed while she tried
to summon the will power to break free. As she
drove around this morning in the cool dawn light
she had told herself that last night had been a
product of too much wine; the fevered desire she
had felt for this man was nothing more than a
mirage, she would have felt the same for any man
if he had happened along while she was in that
aroused state. Well, now she was as sober as a
judge and yet her blood was running faster, her
body shuddering as though she had a high
temperature, her hands were trembling restlessly
as they clung to his shoulders. She wanted to
touch him, to trace the long supple line of his
spine, the muscled breadth of his chest, to frame
his face in her hands and feel his hair twining
through her fingers. Images flashed through her
head and she couldn't shut them out although
one part of her intelligence stood aside, dismayed.

Steve lifted his head at last and she breathed
audibly as she finally found the strength to push
him away and step back, a hand at her mouth,
surprised to find it felt quite normal, it wasn't as
hot and bruised as she had expected.

'Got a better idea of my motives now?' Steve
mocked.

She didn't believe him, her angry eyes said as
much. She didn't have the blatant sex appeal to
make men fall for her at first sight. All her
boyfriends had been slightly tame; she had got to
know them over long periods, learnt to trust them
before she let them kiss her. Trust didn't come

easy to Tess, she had grown up knowing too much about men, especially men as attractive as Steve Houghton. He came out of the same box as her father; both of them were eye-catching, self-assured, sexually dynamic. And not for her.

'Can I eat my breakfast now?' she asked tightly, turning to pick up the tray. She felt her coffee. It was almost cold. She poured herself another which was warmer and went out to eat at the table on the patio in the sunlight.

How long would it take Johnny to switch on his answering machine and hear her message then send her a telegram in reply? She thought back over everything Steve had said, discounting most of it. He had laughed at the idea that he might kidnap her—well, he'd hardly confess to it, would he? He had admitted that he'd invited Franco to join them—but in that case, why pretend that it was a chance meeting? It was perfectly normal to suggest having another man to make up a foursome, why had he lied about it?

When Steve kissed her to prove his point, he'd certainly proved to her that she found him dangerously attractive—he hadn't proved that he felt the same about her. All he had made obvious was that for some reason he wanted her to think he was attracted to her—and she was still sure that Steve had some hidden motive for being at the villa, for wanting her to trust and like him.

When she had eaten her breakfast she went towards the villa and met Steve coming out, in swimming trunks, with a towel over his arm.

'I'm going for a swim—coming? I suppose

Dottie gets up late?' He seemed calm now and Tess eyed him warily. She didn't like the bland look he was wearing; what was behind it?

'I thought I'd ring home sometime this morning,' she said casually, watching him, and saw a leap of reaction in his eyes before he hid it behind drooping lids. 'What's the time difference? I can never remember.'

'An hour, or is it two?' he said casually. 'It's always a mistake to think about home when you're on holiday, you're supposed to get away from it all, not take it with you. Put on a bikini and come and swim.'

'Maybe I will,' she said because she didn't want him to know she had rung Johnny; that might warn him off and she wanted him around when that telegram came and she discovered more about him. Of course, it was just possible that he was strictly who he said he was and there for the reason he gave—but Tess had a deep instinctive suspicion that somehow, somewhere, Steve was lying to her, and she meant to find out if her instincts were on target. She didn't want the rat escaping before she sprang the trap, even if it meant that she had to go on acting the part of the cheese.

'That's better,' Steve said, giving her a warm smile. Warm? she corrected. Self-satisfied was a more accurate description. He thought he had got to her, she was going to be putty in his manipulating hands—but he was mistaken.

She went up to her room and heard Dottie snoring slightly behind her closed door. She would probably sleep until lunchtime and wake up with a headache but no doubt she thought it was well worth it. She had loved her visit to the casino. Tess changed into a bikini and looked ruefully at herself in the mirror. If she had ever wondered if Steve was telling the truth about finding her attractive she only had to look at her reflection; the small, high breasts, flat midriff and narrow hips hardly added up to instant sex appeal. Her layered black hair clung to her scalp, feathering around her small face and giving her profile something of the defiant tension of some Egyptian sculpture; only her large, dark-blue eyes gave her expression and vivacity and they held the same fierce rebellion. Tess didn't like how she looked and she didn't believe Steve did, either. She despised herself because she had a secret hankering to believe the incredible. She wouldn't let herself do that, though. Nobody was making a fool out of her—least of all a man like Steve.

Sighing, she went out into the sunlight and found him streaking from one end of the pool to the other, his tanned body cutting through the water and sending ripples shimmering to the edge of the pool. Tess dived and as she surfaced again found Steve treading water next to her, slicking back the wet black hair from his face with one hand as he smiled at her.

'Race?' he suggested. 'First to finish twenty lengths?'

'You're faster than me—and bigger. Give me a handicap,' Tess said.

'You've already got one,' Steve said drily. 'A chip on your shoulder almost as big as you are.'

She ignored that. 'Give me a length start, okay?'

He wryly agreed but in spite of that, she still saw him flash past her long before she finished and when she hauled herself out of the pool he was sitting on the side grinning at her triumphantly.

'You do like to win, don't you?' Tess said with grim amusement. He looked like a little boy except that there was nothing boyish or little about the width of those tanned shoulders, or the muscles in the tapering thighs.

They settled by the pool on the padded loungers, closing their eyes to bask in the growing heat of the sun, their wet bodies drying within minutes.

'Have you always wanted to write plays?' she asked and Steve began to tell her how he had thought he wanted to act until he realised he didn't have the talent. 'So then I became a journalist but I wasn't much good at either. I was just deciding I wasn't much use at that anything when I had an idea for a play—a radio play. That was the first I ever wrote and by sheer fluke it was accepted and went out on the BBC. I can't say the money was wonderful. Radio doesn't pay huge fees, but it was good training. For a year I wrote radio plays and then I got ambitious.' He laughed. 'I wrote a full-length stage play and I thought it was wonderful The trouble was— nobody seemed to agree with me. It was turned down everywhere. I put it in a drawer and went back to writing for radio.'

'But you didn't stop there?'

'No, I'm pretty tenacious. I had plenty of money, I went away for a month, stayed with some cousins who have a farm in Yorkshire. I wrote another play and by then I'd realised a number of mistakes I'd made with the first. The second was light years away from that. But don't imagine it was snapped up by the first guy who saw it. I rewrote that play for six months but people still seemed doubtful. Then I was asked to write some episodes in a TV soap opera, don't ask which one—I prefer to forget that period in my life. I made far more money and I worked damned hard, they were a friendly bunch on that team—but I was very depressed. I thought I was never going to break into the theatre and that was where I wanted to be. One day—it was one of those dull, grey, rainy days when you wonder why you were ever born—I was typing the latest thrilling episode of the soap and hurling screwed up sheets of paper in all directions, cursing and swearing . . .' He stopped and turned his head to look at her, grimacing. 'Am I boring you?'

'No, go on—I'm fascinated,' Tess said impatiently.

'Well, one day, as I said, I got a 'phone call from my agent who said he might . . . just might, mind you . . . have someone interested in my second play and could I have lunch with him and his contact next day?'

'And you said yes?' Tess said, laughing.

'I don't think I said anything much for five minutes, I just breathed.' Steve's grey eyes smiled at her from beneath his shading hand.

'Was that *Dumb Treason*?' she asked and his face changed; she saw the shade come down over his features as if a hand had drawn a blind at a window.

'No, that was my third play, although it was the second to be staged. The first one is still buried in a drawer somewhere; if I ever find it I'll burn it.'

'Oh, don't do that—it might be better than you think.'

'It couldn't be worse,' Steve said and the shadow had lifted from his face again but she had seen it and she knew that the grim tension she had seen for that moment had had something to do with her father. Had Steve quarrelled with Johnny during the run of the play? Johnny had made it a big hit, he had made Steve famous and rich, as he had made many others famous and rich by acting with them or acting in their productions, but Tess knew the theatre. She knew the darkness under the glittering surface; the envy, the jealousy, the spite which could fester out of sight behind the faces of the beautiful people.

'Do you like my father?' she asked innocently, her eyes closed as though she wasn't really interested.

There was a brief silence, then Steve said coolly: 'Do you?'

Tess hadn't expected that, she took a quick

surprised breath, then rallied. 'I asked first!' she said, pretending to laugh.

'You never mention him unless someone mentions him first,' Steve murmured, and that was easy to answer, she could give a truthful explanation which didn't lead to other questions.

'When I was at school my father was one of the biggest names in the London theatre, all my friends had crushes on him, they were always begging me to have them to tea so that they could meet him. I got sick of being his daughter, of answering questions about him, of knowing that when someone was nice to me it was probably because they hoped I'd invite them home. I suppose it's the same for the children of most famous people.'

'He was a big sex symbol, wasn't he?' Steve said, shifting on the lounger and watching her sideways.

'I suppose so,' she said with conscious irony at all she wasn't saying.

'Did that get to be a bore?'

'It wasn't much fun.'

'Any of your friends try to . . .'

'I never asked them!' Tess said, interrupting that question and flushing, although she was pretty sure the answer to it was yes—some of her teenage friends *had* hung around, hoping Johnny would make a pass, and for all she knew he might have done. She hadn't wanted to know, then— she didn't want to know, now. She hadn't asked many people home if she thought they might meet Johnny; luckily he wasn't there very often

or she would never have had a normal adolescence.

'Johnny was in London a good deal, anyway,'
she said flatly. 'We have a house in the country,
that was where Hal and I grew up. My father
wasn't there most of the time.'

'Were your parents separated?'

'Legally? No. But in every other sense of the
word,' she said before she knew what she was
saying and then bit her lip angrily. How had he
got her to admit that? Steve had talked frankly
about himself and his own life and somehow she
had slowly begun to loosen up too. Had he
planned it that way?

'It must be rough on your mother being
married to a man who shows up in so many other
women's dreams,' Steve said softly and she very
nearly answered, then she closed her eyes and
settled herself on her stomach on the padded
lounger.

'I'm going to take a nap now,' she said firmly,
and this time Steve took the hint and was silent.
Tess heard the rustle of the trees around them,
the sound of Steve breathing, the call of birds
flying over head. She tried to sleep but her mind
was too active. Steve had said he had been a
journalist—and a bad one. She had a strong
feeling that he had been a very good one—his
quiet questions just now had been, she suspected,
an expert interrogation by someone who knew
exactly what answers he wanted and was feeling
his way to getting them.

But what was he after? Everyone knew that

Johnny was promiscuous; he had never made any secret of it, it wouldn't be a scandal because nobody would be surprised. Tess herself probably knew less about her father's affairs than the public did because whenever she saw some reference to his private life in gossip columns she quickly turned the page, she never read that stuff, it sickened her.

Of course, she might be hyper-sensitive to any mention of her father. Steve might not be trying to pump her at all; he might have been simply curious about her background and how she saw Johnny. It would be a human reaction, and Tess would have decided that that explained Steve's constant prodding and probing about Johnny if she hadn't been so afraid that she was trying to believe that because she was getting more and more involved with Steve.

CHAPTER FIVE

DOTTIE finally staggered downstairs around noon and when she had revived herself with some strong black coffee suggested that they should go into Nice to do some shopping and have a late lunch. Tess glanced at Steve, her eyes thoughtful, as he agreed calmly that that would be a good idea.

'Shouldn't your car be fixed by now? We'll call in at the garage and see if they've finished working on it, shall we?'

'Want to get rid of me, do you?' he drawled, unsurprised, but Dottie was far from eager to see him leave. She threw her friend an accusing look, pouting.

'Tess didn't mean that,' she wrongly claimed. 'Did you, Tess? It's fun having you here and Tess and I like company. We aren't conventional—after all, we can chaperon each other, there's no problem, and there's plenty of room. Yesterday was marvellous. I can't remember when I had so much fun.'

Tess thought of the telegram she was waiting for and shrugged. As soon as her father replied she would know for certain whether Steve was genuine or not, she could wait until then.

'Franco suggested we try some wind surfing off the Neptune beach,' Dottie confided as they drove off from the villa.

'I thought you mentioned shopping in Nice,' Tess said drily. She might have known that Dottie had some other motive for wanting to go there. 'Franco's meeting us there, I suppose?'

'That's right,' Dottie said defiantly, her long hair blowing around her face as the car turned into the village high street. She was like a ricocheting bullet, spinning from one man to another, bouncing off each without a halt. Her bright eyes told Tess to mind her own business and Tess held her tongue; if Dottie chose to live like that who was she to stop her? Sometimes she wondered why Dottie inevitably picked the wrong men but even Dottie herself probably didn't know that. She had always been the same as long as Tess could remember; they had known each other for years and all that time Dottie had been reckless, restless and volatile while Tess had been watchful and self-contained, and which approach to life was the wiser Tess wasn't going to guess. She knew her own character had been slightly warped by her bitter distrust of her father, and every other man she met. What had shaped Dottie?

Tess pulled up at the garage. 'Shall I go in and see if your car is ready?' she asked Steve with outward innocence and he gave her a dry smile.

'No, I'll go.'

She watched his long legs cover the ground rapidly as he strode into the shadowy interior where several men were working. The afternoon heat had thickened into brazen insistence, Tess was wearing sunglasses and had smoothed suntan oil into her bare arms and shoulders where her thin cotton dress left her skin exposed.

'Isn't it hot?' she groaned and Dottie agreed absently.

'Why are you trying to get rid of Steve? Don't you like him? You seemed to be getting on well,' she complained, then added blatantly: 'If he goes, what am I going to do about Franco? I can't go out with him leaving you at the villa, but if you come with us . . . well, three's a crowd.'

Tess watched Steve coming back towards them, the sun glinting on his black hair. 'I don't think we're going to lose Steve just yet,' she said with irony.

'Not ready yet?' she asked him as he opened the door and got back into the car, and he threw her an amused look, recognising the sarcastic note in her voice.

'I'm afraid it was more complicated than they'd thought—they've promised to have it ready tomorrow, though.'

'Oh, *good*!' Tess said, starting the engine. 'That *must* be a relief to you.'

As she drove off, Steve asked casually, 'Done any windsurfing before?'

'No, but I'm longing to,' Dottie said eagerly.

'What about you, Tess?' he asked, leaning forward so that his cheek almost brushed her bare arm. Dottie was sitting beside her and Steve was in the back; Tess had made sure of that by saying that she didn't want Steve commenting on her driving the way he had yesterday. Steve had pointed out that she had been drunk yesterday, but she had insisted, pretending to laugh, and Dottie had imagined that she was helping Tess play some elaborate game with Steve, the sort of game Dottie understood and played herself.

'I've tried it but I kept falling off the board and I swallowed too much of the sea to enjoy it,' she said, shifting so that her arm was further from his face.

'I'll teach you,' he promised. 'Are you a slow learner?'

Her eyes met his in the driving mirror, she felt herself flushing. There was wicked amusement in his smile.

'I'll just sunbathe,' she said crossly; she had hated her only experience of windsurfing, it was harder than it looked and very undignified when you kept lurching off into the sea.

'Oh, we can't have that,' said Steve. 'Don't worry, I'll enjoy teaching you.'

Dottie giggled and Tess put her foot down on the accelerator; furious with both of them.

She protested again later, when they were on the beach after having lunch at a restaurant in the old quarter of Nice. Franco had taken Dottie off to learn how to windsurf; Tess had been watching them lazily as she smoothed more suntan oil into her shoulders, smiling as Dottie wobbled and fell off with a splash which could be heard on the beach. Her wail of fury a second later was even louder and Tess began to laugh, but her amusement vanished when Steve sat up and said: 'Come on, you've been lazy long enough! You'll soon pick up the way to balance on the board, you're light on your feet, you should be a natural windsurfer.'

'No, I don't want to,' Tess refused, screwing the top back on her suntan oil and lying down on her stomach.

Steve knelt on her mattress and slapped her lightly, on her bikini-clad bottom. 'Coward!'

'Don't do that!' She half turned to glare at him and he suddenly scooped her up and set off down the beach with Tess wriggling and kicking in his arms. She got angrier as she heard people laughing, they were attracting attention from the others on the beach and Steve's macho act was popular with their audience, if not with Tess.

She threw him an angry upward stare and he eyed her with complacent mockery; the power of his lean, muscled body beyond her ability to resist it. She sensed the kick he got out of handling her slight, skimpily clad body with such easy mastery, and vibrated with resentment.

'If you don't put me down I'll bite you,' she promised.

'Oh, in that case,' he said coolly and dropped her.

She fell with a shriek, landing in water just deep enough to let her swim away, and was furious enough to grab at Steve's ankle and yank him off balance. Tess was gone before he got himself together again, but she heard him coming after her with an easy crawl and put on more speed to get away from him. He was faster, though. He caught up with her and grabbed her; their bodies tangling in smooth, wet coils, his thighs deftly enclosing her to stop her escaping, one arm clamped around her midriff. She felt his fingers brush her breast and gasped in shock; his grey eyes glanced down into hers with awareness.

'Does everything scare you? Who'd have thought you were such a little scaredy cat?' he murmured, his lips brushing her ear as she turned her head away, her black hair floating on the buoyant sea. 'That's what you remind me of—a small, spitting, frightened black cat.'

'Be careful, this cat has claws,' she said huskily, digging her nails into his shoulder.

'That hurts!' he muttered, letting go of her, and she swam back towards the shoreline, the glitter of sunlight on water making her eyes wince. Steve was just behind her and as her feet touched the bottom so that she could stand up he straightened, too, the salty water running down his body; glistening in the black curls of hair growing up the centre of the brown chest. He looked down at her with mock menace, pushing her damp hair back from her face, and Tess met his stare defiantly.

'You're not such an iceberg as you'd like me to think,' Steve said. 'Or is it yourself you're trying to convince? What did that father of yours do to you? All men aren't like him, you know.'

'What have you got against my father?' she asked; at once wary, suspicious. 'Are you *sure* you're a playwright? You're not still a journalist, by any chance?'

His mouth twisted crookedly in a wry smile, but his eyes were even warier than her own, and

Tess saw that; so that what he said wasn't all she read into his reactions. 'No, I'm not still a journalist and I was a damned bad one even when I was working on a Fleet Street paper. Most stories I covered bored me—if I got interested and wrote an in-depth piece the sub-editors always spiked it, they always wanted formula stuff, and I found that tedious.'

Tess considered him sarcastically, her feet still in the shallow water at the edge of the beach, her slender body drying already in the sunlight.

'You didn't tell me what you have against my father,' she pointed out. 'I'm not completely dumb, you know.'

'Why should I answer your questions when you'll never answer mine?'

'Stalemate, isn't it?' she said.

Steve glanced away, then smiled. 'Dottie's doing fine now—look!'

Tess followed his gaze and saw Dottie skimming along on the sailboard, her long hair streaming like a banner on the wind. 'That's amazing,' she agreed. 'I'm impressed. Franco must be a good teacher—maybe I'll ask him to teach me.'

'That's adding insult to injury,' Steve said. 'You might try giving me a chance—in one direction at least.'

She flushed at the sardonic note and the underlying implication. 'I like to look before I leap,' she justified.

'That had dawned on me—I never met a more distrustful female. You question everything and believe nothing, I suppose you'd describe that as modern thinking but you must waste a lot of time and energy that way.'

'It's safer, though,' she said and he gave a faint sigh.

'You worry me, you're so busy making sure you don't make any mistakes that you may end up not having lived at all.'

'I won't bite at that old line,' Tess informed him. 'That's been spun to me too many times before.'

Dottie splashed up to them, flushed and triumphant. 'That was ace! I loved it. You ought to try it, Tess, really, you'd have a marvellous time once you got the hang of it. It seems hard at first but it's like riding a bike, you only have to get your balance and then it's really easy. I fell in a dozen times before I managed to learn but it was worth it.'

Franco paddled up, his arm over the sailboard and the gaudy red sail floating on the water. 'I give you a lesson, Tess?' he offered.

'Well,' she said uncertainly, half inclined to try it, and Dottie urged her to go ahead, but Steve intervened and insisted that if anyone was going to teach her it was him. Dottie winked at her and Franco amiably pushed the sailboard towards Steve.

For the next hour Tess kept attempting to escape, she found it impossible to pull the heavy sail up out of the water which seemed to drag it down and even when she had finally managed to raise the sail she couldn't stay balanced on the

board when the wind took the sail and sent her
scudding sideways. She would set off, leaning
slightly outwards, and suddenly her feet would
slip on the wet board and she would be flung off
into the sea. Her midriff and stomach muscles
ached from the constant hard contact with the
water; her arms ached from manœuvring the
heavy sail, her calves ached from the tension of
keeping her balance, her toes gripping the board.

'I've had enough,' she wailed to Steve as he
tried to get her to climb back after yet another
spill.

'One more effort, then we'll stop,' he said, and
with the prospect of being able to relax in front of
her, Tess finally managed to stay on for five
minutes, skimming away from Steve and feeling
the friction of the wind rippling her hair and
rushing over body. When she toppled into the
waves that time she bobbed about, propelling the
board in front of her, making for the beach,
tingling with triumph. She hadn't believed she
could do it, and when she met Steve in the gentle
surf she grinned delightedly at him.

'I told you so,' he said, amused.

'The four most maddening words in the
language,' Tess panted, still winded from her
efforts.

'Maybe—but I hope it's proved something to
you,' he murmured and walked with her up the
pebbled beach when they had handed in the
sailboard to the boy in charge. Tess wondered
precisely what Steve had meant by that, but
decided not to ask, partly because she guessed he

wanted her to and partly because she was afraid of the answer.

They all had dinner at a small Chinese restaurant specialising in Vietnamese cooking, as Chinese restaurants in France often do, where Cantonese duck in plum sauce can be found on the same menu as more unfamiliar dishes from rural Vietnam. Their table was crowded with a dozen little bowls of interesting food from which they took tiny amounts with chopsticks; tasting each one in turn, from salted water chestnuts to chicken in lemon sauce with noodles.

Franco told them that he was a cartoonist as well as a singer; he drew portraits of them all on the day's menu and Steve asked if he could keep it. Franco called the restaurant manager over; the man stared impassively at the four small cartoons and Steve told him he wanted to keep the menu. It sounded odd to hear the Vietnamese speaking rapid French but he seemed to be agreeing. Steve pushed a French bank note into his hand and himself pocketed the menu. They half bowed to each other soberly and the manager trod softly away. The two candles lighting their corner table flickered and made faint smoke trails in the shadows, Tess gazed at the small flames, feeling sleepy and oddly happy. Dottie and Franco were arguing over some film they had both seen, Steve was glancing at the bill which the manager had handed him. Tess ached pleasurably, aware of every muscle in her back and shoulders after her tussle with the sailboard, her skin glowing with the heat of the sun. She was filled with that

MAIL THIS CARD TO RECEIVE 4 ROMANCE NOVELS PLUS A VALUABLE GIFT

FREE

Tear off and mail this card today.

EXTRAS:

- OUR FREE NEWSLETTER HEART TO HEART
- OUR FREE MAGAZINE ROMANCE DIGEST
- SPECIAL-EDITION HARLEQUIN BESTSELLERS TO PREVIEW FOR TEN DAYS
- NO OBLIGATION TO BUY EVER

SAVINGS:

$1.60 OFF THE TOTAL RETAIL PRICE. PAY NOTHING MORE FOR SHIPPING AND HANDLING.

SAVINGS DATA CARD

Notice: Mail this card today to get 4 Free Harlequin Presents novels plus a FREE valuable gift. You'll get 8 brand-new Presents novels every month as they come off the presses for only $1.75 each (a savings of $0.20 off the retail price) with no extra charges for shipping and handling. You can return a shipment and cancel anytime. The 4 FREE books and valuable gift are yours to keep!

108-CIP-CAJ5

(Please PRINT in ink)

☐ MS
☐ MISS
☐ MRS.

FIRST NAME _____ INITIAL ___ LAST NAME _____

ADDRESS _____ APT. ___

CITY OR TOWN _____ STATE ___ ZIP CODE ___

NOTE: IF YOU MAIL THIS CARD TODAY YOU'LL GET A SECOND MYSTERY GIFT FREE

Offer limited to one household and not valid for present subscribers. Prices subject to change.

special contentment which comes from a day spent actively in the open air with people you like; she was reluctant to move from the quiet little restaurant, with its coloured lanterns and embroidered scarlet dragons on the wall, and a stream of non-stop Chinese music on the tannoy as a restful background noise.

Steve counted out franc notes and stood up. A waiter rushed to open the door, bowing them out. Tess gave a faint shiver; the night air seemed cool on her overheated skin. They said goodnight to Franco who was driving back to Cap d'Antibes and the Eden-Roc, where he was staying, and then they drove to the villa. Although it was late at night the roads were still crowded as holiday-makers flowed from one resort to another along the glittering coast, but as they rose into the hills they found emptier roads and fewer cars.

Steve was driving and Tess sat beside him, her head back on the seat, her eyes on the stars high above them; a frosted brilliance in the way they shone through the cloudless night sky.

Dottie was half asleep in the back, yawning from time to time, and saying nothing. Tess didn't want to talk either, she didn't want to change her mood, she felt like someone trying to walk on eggshells without breaking them. She couldn't ever remember feeling this fragile, elusive happiness and she was terrified of feeling it smash.

When they had parked the car on the drive and gone into the villa Dottie mumbled 'Good night,' and almost groped her way upstairs with slitted

eyes like a sleepwalker. Tess and Steve watched
her in silence; Tess knew she ought to go up to
bed too, she knew it was crazy to stand there,
waiting for something, but for what? For Steve to
kiss her? Yes, of course, but it wasn't that
obvious or that simple. She was waiting for a
moment she had thought would never happen—
for a happiness she had imagined she would
never know.

Steve looked down at her, his black pupils
dilated, glittering like the frosty stars she had
seen in the sky just now, and suddenly she felt he
was just as far away as those stars, as out of reach
to her; too brilliant, too remote, she had felt him
deceptively close and attainable when he was
really millions of miles away.

'Good night,' she said hurriedly, her voice low.

'Coffee?' he said as she turned away.

'No, it will keep me awake.'

'Do you really want to sleep?' Steve asked in
a voice which sent fire through her veins
because she knew he meant: to sleep alone, to
leave him and go up to her silent room with
only her own company, and Tess didn't want
that but she knew it was the safest course all
the same. 'It was a good day,' he said in the
same smoky voice, so close that she felt the
warmth of his breath on her bare nape. He bent
and she felt his lips there too, gently brushing
her skin, offering much more than the light
touch he was giving at the moment.

'Yes, but I'm tired,' she said, putting her foot
on the first stair.

'Stop running away,' he mocked but he didn't try to stop her.

'I'm not running,' Tess said with tired humour. 'I'm walking—I haven't got the energy to run, not tonight. Try again tomorrow; by then I'll be myself again and you'll get the clip on the ear you deserve.'

He laughed and let her go, watching her all the way until she had gone into her room and closed the door on him and the restless, beckoning eyes she was only too aware of, although she didn't once look back.

She fell asleep the second her head touched the pillow, but woke up towards dawn feeling very thirsty. She must have slept restlessly, her bed was a tangle of sheets which she had kicked to the bottom. If she dreamt she couldn't remember it, her sleep must have been heavy, if energetic.

She padded downstairs in her short cotton nightie to get a drink from the kitchen. There wasn't a sound from the other rooms, Dottie and Steve must be fast asleep. She stood by the kitchen window staring out into the dawn-lit garden hearing the first waking calls of the birds, drinking a glass of mineral water which was ice-cold from the fridge.

She thought of Steve's husky, inviting voice last night and closed her eyes, trembling. She didn't want to feel this way; it would be insanity. He wouldn't mean anything by making love to her; he came from a world where going to bed together was as casual and meaningless as sharing a cigarette. Tess wasn't that casual. She would mean it; she wouldn't just be giving her body, she would be giving the love she had never given anyone—and there was so much of it hidden inside her. This was the first time she had ever felt—not that she loved—but that she *wanted* to love, she ached to feel, to spend herself like a miser suddenly showering handfuls of long-treasured gold into open hands. She kept telling herself to be careful, to remember how her father treated women, telling herself that Steve was the same kind of man. But she wasn't so sure about that now. Steve wasn't an echo of her father—he was far too real to her after yesterday. She was getting to know so much about him; it might sound crazy but she felt she knew him better than she had ever known her father. Johnny had always been a distant figure—Steve had come close, very close. He wasn't a black outline, he was a three-dimensional man to her; she knew what made him laugh, what he liked to eat, what he felt about world affairs and politics and music and books. They had talked for hours and she had constantly discovered new things about him.

She had never known a man as well as she now knew Steve—putting down the empty glass she laughed at that thought. Was it really true? Yes, she told herself in sudden soberness. True—and rather sad. Most girls learn about men from their fathers and brothers. Tess hadn't learnt anything much from Johnny, except to despise and distrust him. Her brother was much older than herself; Hal had got married while Tess was still at school, she had been an aunt by the time she was nineteen. She loved her brother, it was true, but she didn't know that much about him as a person, she hadn't been old enough while he lived at home to see Hal as anything but the big brother who teased and was boisterous with her. When she was an adult herself she and Hal became friends in a new way, but his close relationship with his wife was always what occupied Hal, Tess had always been an outsider.

Last night, though, she had felt she was closer to Steve than she had been to any other member of the opposite sex. Was that why she had felt so happy? She had been poised on the brink of some momentous discovery, she hadn't wanted to rush or grab at it. She had wanted to prolong that blissful anticipation, that was why she had gone to bed while Steve's eyes invited her not to go alone.

She walked across the hall to go back upstairs to shower and dress, she knew she wouldn't get back to sleep. Halfway towards the stairs she stopped, suddenly seeing Steve in the sitting-room. The glass door was closed, he was lying on the white couch, his head pillowed on a jade green cushion and his long body sprawled in sleep.

Tess tiptoed over to the door and softly opened it. He must have been reading and fallen asleep where he was, she saw a leather-bound book open on the carpet. She didn't make a sound as she crossed the room; the deep-piled carpet swallowed up her footsteps. She ought to go, let the poor man sleep, but she had a peculiar craving to see him in this defenceless, vulnerable state—it would tell her so much about him and she wanted to know everything about Steve. Asleep he wouldn't be on his guard; holding up a mask in front of his face, hiding anything or trying to deceive; there would be no performance, only a man asleep.

She stood by the couch, hardly breathing in case she woke him, staring down at the strongly modelled face, the rise and fall of his powerful chest. He slept deeply, breathing with regular ease, his mouth slightly open, his features relaxed, smoothed out, the thick black lashes clustered on his cheek, his skin warmly flushed.

Tenderness welled up inside her, she wanted to touch him, brush a hand over the blue-black hair which sleep had ruffled and tousled, lay her fingers on the warm brown skin at his throat where his shirt lay open, feel the gently beating blue vein at the side of his neck.

His right arm hung down off the couch, his open hand brushing the carpet as if the leather-bound book had dropped from his hand in the instant that he fell asleep. What had he been reading? Tess wondered, bending to pick up the book.

It wasn't a printed book at all, though; it was a thickly leaved ruled exercise book bound in black leather, and her first glance saw neat flowing shorthand. Steve hadn't been reading—he had been writing. A play? she thought then dismissed that idea because the pages were too crammed with symbols. The lay-out was wrong for it to be a play. Tess was about to close the book and put it down when her eye caught her own name. It leapt out of the sea of words and she stiffened. She had done a six months' secretarial course in the sixth form at school; she hadn't kept up her shorthand but she knew enough to read Steve's notes, as her eye travelled rapidly over the page on which her own name appeared—appeared not once but several times in that paragraph.

Steve had been noting down one of the conversations they had had; she remembered the questions he had asked, the answers she had given. He had memorised her reply and there it was—she read it through slowly, her skin turning cold and a dull tension making her spine rigid.

Why was Steve keeping notes on everything she said? Trembling, she began to flip through the back pages; her name showed up on every page she looked at and she felt her knees give under her, she staggered back into an armchair and sat down with Steve's notebook clutched in her shaking hand. She hadn't noticed a glass balanced on the arm of the chair, her elbow knocked it and it spun across the room with a clatter which made Steve start and wake up, his eyes opening, his face abruptly alert as he glanced around the room.

He saw Tess almost at once; surprise showed in his grey eyes, then a smile crept into them and was repeated in his mouth which curved at the corners.

'Hallo, I was just dreaming about you,' he said softly, holding out his hand.

Tess looked at it with bitter distaste. 'Were you

really? Were you dreaming that I'd found your notebook and discovered that you kept secret notes on everything I say?'

She was watching him, she saw the stiffening of his long body, the narrowed appraisal of his eyes, the sudden masked blankness of his face while he tried to work out what to say.

She flung the notebook at him, catching him in the midriff and making him curl up like a salted snail, with a winded gasp. Tess didn't wait to hear the lies he was inventing—she fled barefoot from the room and Steve, but however fast she ran she couldn't ever escape from herself and the sick misery filling every corner of her mind.

CHAPTER SIX

SHE ran so fast that she was halfway up the stairs before she heard Steve coming after her. He had been too sleepy to think quickly but his legs were longer than hers and he came with speed. She only just reached her room in time to slam the door and shoot the bolt; Steve's weight thudded into it a fraction too late as he hurled himself from the top step. The whole door shook and Tess backed, wondering if he meant to break it down like the hero of some film. She wouldn't put it past him and was in such a furious temper that she half-hoped he would; violence would satisfy something explosive inside her too.

'Tess!' Steve had paused to think, though; his hand rattled the handle on the door, he banged on the wooden panels. 'Tess, I don't know what you're thinking but you're jumping to conclusions, you didn't give me a chance to explain.'

'Clear off,' she said, her voice rough with salt. She was so angry she could break things—she had promised herself long ago that no man would ever make her cry, but Steve had managed it. She rubbed a shaky hand over her wet eyes. Fool, she told herself. This must be the first and last time; it mustn't ever happen again. You couldn't trust men—when would she finally understand that? She had told herself often enough in the past, yet

Steve had managed to get through all her defences in a few days.

'Open this door—I can't shout through it. How can we talk if you won't let me see you?'

Tess was seeing herself—all too clearly. She eyed her reflection with self-disgust; in the pale dawn light she looked like a red-eyed little mouse who's on the run from a cat that has just had it pinned into a corner.

'Tess,' Steve said. 'Okay, stay there, but listen. Tess? Are you listening?' He waited but she disdained to answer. She walked into the shower and noisily ran the water, drowning out his voice. He could talk to the door—but she wasn't listening. She dropped her cotton nightie on the floor and stepped under the cool water, jumping at the first impact of it on her hot skin. She pretended not to be listening but she couldn't help wondering if Steve was still out there, talking to himself; she hoped he was—she'd like to catch him making a fool of himself.

That was a faint hope. Men like Steve don't make fools of themselves—they just do that to others, but they can't do it to you unless you let them and in that sense *you're* the one making a fool of yourself, she told her reflection in the bathroom mirror. She stepped out of the shower and began to towel herself. What did he mean to do with those notes? Publish them in some magazine article? Was he a journalist, after all? His notes had been a word for word reproduction of their talk; an aid to his memory so that he could prove she had actually said whatever he printed?

She walked back into her bedroom, naked, and began to search for something to wear. She was in such an irritable state that she hated every garment she possessed, throwing them aside with impatience after one look.

Something scrabbled at her half-closed shutters and she looked into the mirror in surprise—had a bird just crashed into the window? Her heart went into her throat as she saw a foot wearing a cream-coloured training shoe; it kicked and the shutters flew backwards, rattling. Tess suddenly realised what was going on and ran towards the window to pull the shutters shut again, then halted in confusion remembering that she wasn't wearing a stitch of clothing. She backtracked to snatch up her towel, wrapping it around her so that it covered her from breast to knee. The brief delay had cost her the chance to keep Steve out; as she ran back towards the window again he came flying through the air like Tarzan, his arms raised to catch the sill above her room, his feet coming through the open window with his body following them, as if he was limbo dancing. He didn't land too brilliantly, of course; he crashed to a heap on the floor at her feet and looked up, laughing.

Tess wasn't amused. 'What the hell do you think you're doing? You might have been killed—what a stupid thing to do!' He must have swung from his own balcony next door, balancing on the iron rail while he pried her shutters open. It had been a risky, dangerous operation and she was so angry that she forgot for a second her other reasons for being antagonistic to him, then she remembered and walked towards the door. 'Get out of my room,' she said, pulling back the bolt and hoping that her sheer rage might make him go.

He sat upright, put his arms around his knees and considered her without speaking.

'You aren't pulling the wool over my eyes again,' she said, holding the door open. 'I read those notes, I don't know what you plan to do with them but if you print a word I said I'll have my lawyer speak to the Press Council and lay charges against you. You didn't tell me you were interviewing me; it was a private conversation.' Her voice was shaking now and her face was flushed. 'I didn't know you were trying to pump me for information about my father.' She had suspected often enough but he had lulled her suspicions to sleep. 'You're a lying snake.' It made it much worse that she had begun by suspecting him and ended by being ready to fall in love. 'Sneaky, underhand rat,' she hissed.

'Tess,' Steve said, getting to his feet.

'Low-down, two-faced, despicable worm.'

'You read what I'd written—didn't you realise I was just writing down everything you said so that I wouldn't forget it? Any reason why I shouldn't keep notes of what you like to eat, what books you read, what colour your eyes are when you're smiling?'

Tess felt her throat hurt and Steve took a step towards her. She refused to soften, eyeing him with contempt.

'Phoney, sweet-talking bastard,' she offered in

a voice she couldn't stop from trembling. 'Don't give me any of that stuff, not any more, I don't want to hear any of it.'

'I keep a diary,' Steve said, coming closer. 'Don't you?'

'That wasn't a diary!'

'It isn't divided into individual days; some days I have nothing to write in there, other days I write pages of stuff. I date each entry, that way I don't waste pages. Surely you must have realised I was keeping a record of whatever happened to me each day?'

She faltered, scowling, uncertain suddenly. What if he was telling the truth? 'I didn't notice anything of the kind,' she said though.

'How good's your shorthand?' Steve asked and he was now so close that when he put out a hand and quietly closed the door again she was too confused by his proximity to think of arguing.

'Good enough to know that a lot of that stuff was about me!'

'Exactly,' he said in huskily intimate tones that made her bones turn to water. Steve saw the weakness in her eyes and put out a hand.

'Don't you touch me!' Tess backed and found the door behind her.

'You called me some very unpleasant names,' Steve said softly, a curl of satisfaction lifting the edges of his hard mouth, as he placed a hand on either side of her head, trapping her.

'I didn't see anything about you in those notes,' she thought aloud. 'It was all quotes from me and a lot of it was about my father.'

A flicker of impatience crossed his face; one of his hands dropped, so fast that she didn't guess what he meant to do until he had snatched her towel away. With a gasp of shock Tess dived under his arm to grab the quilt from the bed, but she didn't have time to wind herself into it. Steve's body collided with hers and she sprawled across the bed with Steve falling on top of her.

She gave a startled, upward glance, beginning to shake violently; the weight of his muscled body was more pleasure than pain, and angry though she still was, she was confused, divided, half excited by the contact, half afraid of it, and of how it made her feel.

Steve looked down into her eyes, breathing thickly. Tess couldn't speak, could barely breathe. His mouth searched downward as she shakily turned her head away, unable to hold his stare; she felt his lips on her cheek, then they caught her mouth and took it hungrily.

Tess closed her eyes; she felt so hot suddenly that the sheets clung to her naked skin, she touched him and shuddered with desire, her mouth melting under the exploration of his kiss, her body boneless, silky with passion, arching up towards him while he touched her with restless, wandering hands.

The sudden opening of the door was like a douche of cold water, they stiffened, springing apart as they looked round.

Dottie's face was comic—if they had been in any mood to find it funny—she was pink and flustered, her eyes like saucers. 'Sorry,' she gabbled, retreating 'I . . . oh, sorry . . .'

The door slammed shut again and they heard the scamper of her bare feet as she shot back to her room. Steve said something violent through his teeth as he sat up, raking back his tousled hair. He was dark red and there was a little tic beating at the side of his cheek.

Tess pulled the quilt over her naked body, shivering. She felt as if she had come back to earth from a journey to another planet; her mind was still there, she had emotional jet lag, with some disastrous physical side-effects.

'Not the best timing in the world,' Steve said with harsh amusement as he began to recover from the shock.

'Please,' Tess said. 'Go away.' What on earth had Dottie thought? What a stupid question, she told herself; you know what Dottie thought and she was a hundred per cent right. Another two minutes and Dottie would have interrupted something a good deal more embarrassing.

'Damn Dottie, what did she have to wake up so early for? The first time she's got up before midday and it had to be today,' Steve said, lounging on the side of the bed but not trying to touch her again, although he wasn't taking his eyes off her and she sensed that he was watching every flicker of expression in her face. But then he always was, wasn't he? Right from the first moment he arrived he had been watching her and, no doubt, writing down every syllable she uttered in that so-called 'diary', and Tess wished she knew what went on behind his grey eyes. What was he thinking about as he stared at her so fixedly?

'Don't shake like that,' he suddenly said with rough impatience.

'I'm not' she denied childishly through chattering teeth. Was that shock? She'd heard somewhere that shock made you feel cold.

'So Dottie saw us,' Steve grimaced. 'So what? It won't have turned her hair white; she won't have nightmares about it. She's a sophisticated young woman, not a nun.'

'It was embarrassing, all the same,' Tess said; not so much because Steve had been making love to her as because she had been as naked as Salome when the last veil dropped, and, however sophisticated Dottie might be—was, undoubtedly—she had visibly been taken aback when she saw them. In all the time Dottie had known her, she had never walked in on a scene like that. Dottie herself was far too discreet for it to have happened the other way around, and Tess knew how *she* would feel if she opened a door and saw another woman naked in the arms of a man on a bed. She wouldn't be shocked but she would certainly vanish as quickly as Dottie had done.

'Would you mind going? I want to get dressed,' she said politely, as though he was a stranger.

'We've got to talk, there's something we have to say,' Steve said.

'No, no more, please.' She was on the point of tears again.

'We aren't too good at words,' Steve said. 'We get on much better when we don't use them, have you noticed? Whenever I try to talk to you I feel

I'm trying to break through some wall you've put up round yourself. It's there now; I can almost see it.'

'Don't touch me,' she cried out as he moved towards her and he looked down at her, his hands curled and impotent at his side, his face angry.

'You must have had an appalling childhood to be like this about men,' he said in a voice he tried to make gentle. 'How old were you when your mother and father first split up?'

'They never split up,' Tess said. 'They're still married, Johnny still visits her—he still says they're married, anyway.'

'And what does she say?'

'She has never breathed a word against him, not to me, not to Hal—if you only listened to her you'd believe that they had a perfect marriage.' She saw the disbelief and cynicism in his face as he smiled.

'But I'm willing to bet that she made sure you knew every detail of every affair he ever had; she cried just loudly enough for you to hear her, she was brave and suffering through her smiles. Oh, Tess, it's an old pattern—the children used as pawns in a vicious game of matrimonial warfare.'

Trembling with rage, she broke out: 'That's my mother you're talking about, remember! I know her better than you do!'

'She's your mother, but she's Johnny's wife and he's given her a hundred reasons for hating him.'

'You don't know her! She doesn't hate him, heaven only knows why, and even if she did why

should she lie to me about how she feels? I've
often asked why she doesn't divorce him, she
knows I wouldn't be hurt or shocked if she did.'

'I thought she never discussed him with you?'
he asked drily.

'I've sometimes tried to talk about it, but she
won't, she's too loyal, and she never tried to use
Hal or myself as pawns. How could she, anyway?
We barely know our father, he doesn't mean a
thing to either of us—he was never there, it was
my mother who brought us up and kept the home
together. Johnny just descended on us from time
to time with presents, he didn't care whether we
knew about his affairs or not, I often wondered if
he remembered we existed while he was in
London and busy with his latest play.'

'All the same, you were his children, as well as
hers,' Steve said quietly, still watching her
flushed face. 'Just by keeping you firmly on her
side of the family battlefield, she was using you
against him. He's a human being, he must care
about his own flesh and blood.'

Tess laughed with savage irony. 'He's not a
human being—he's an actor and he'd be the first
to deny that he's mere flesh and blood. Haven't
you heard? Johnny Linden is one of the gods;
someone once did a survey of the most-
photographed men and women of the post-war
years and Johnny came very high up the list.'

Steve took a long breath, shaking his head.
'And you claim he doesn't mean a thing to you!
Good God, Tess, the man has practically hand-
hewn you; your whole character, the way you

live, the way you think, comes from being Johnny Linden's daughter. You're warped about men because you don't trust your father, you're bitter and angry about him but he fascinates you, doesn't he?'

'The way snakes fascinate, perhaps,' Tess said furiously. 'Maybe that's what I . . .' she broke off what she had incautiously been about to say, but Steve's eyes narrowed and he watched her with cool comprehension.

'What you see in me?' he asked in dry illumination. 'I had a strong suspicion that you'd tarred me with the same brush as your father.'

'I don't want to talk about him! Why are you so determined to get me to tell you all this? Will you write all this up in your alleged "diary" the minute you're alone? I don't trust you an inch— how do I even know your real name? Where's your passport? Prove that you're Steve Houghton, show me a letter from my father renting you this villa, tell me why you're so interested in my family.'

She had a lot more to say to him, but her voice was shaking audibly and she was trembling inside the quilt, she was afraid to say any more and stopped abruptly. Steve was looking at her with a strange expression in his eyes; she didn't know if it was confusion or bewilderment but it made him slowly walk away towards the door before he answered. Perhaps he hadn't realised how deep her suspicions of him ran, perhaps he was taken aback to discover that she wasn't fooled by his lovemaking into swallowing every lie he told her?

'I've got my passport in my room,' he said curtly. 'You can see it any time you like.'

'Does it describe you as a playwright?' Tess demanded. 'Or as a journalist?'

Steve opened the bedroom door. 'As a journalist, actually,' he admitted in a cool voice. 'It's five years old and it was accurate then— when I get a new one I'll change the job description.'

'Oh, sure,' Tess said and he gave her a brief, hard look before he went, letting the door slam behind him.

Tess went back into the shower and showered again; she felt she needed to, her skin felt like glass with fingerprints all over it. She scrubbed her body with a loofah; she despised him, he had betrayed her. She had always sworn she wouldn't be taken in by a man like that but when it came to it her own sensuality had been too strong, she had wanted Steve, she couldn't pretend he had used force, he hadn't needed to, had he?

Dressed in jeans and a clean blue sweatshirt she looked at herself with contempt. Maybe she had more of her father in her than she had imagined; why hadn't that occurred to her? She might not look anything like him, but perhaps he had passed on to her that weakness of the flesh which led him from woman to woman? She hadn't stampeded from man to man—yet. But she hadn't been able to fight the violent sexual need she felt for Steve, a heated desire she had never felt for any other man. In the past she hadn't let herself get that involved with anyone who might arouse such feelings; she had played safe, picked men she instinctively knew wouldn't be a temptation, or a risk. She had known on sight that she should keep Steve at arms' length; he had 'handle with care' written all over him.

She went downstairs, keyed up in case she found Steve waiting for her, but it was Dottie who was in the kitchen drinking coffee and eating a croissant. Tess went pink at the sight of her and Dottie plunged into gabbled speech, 'There's fresh coffee, I didn't have orange juice, we're out of oranges and the croissants are rubbery, they've gone stale. I suppose we ought to get some more; the bread may be okay.'

'No, I think I'll go for a drive, pick up some groceries and have a *petit dejeuner* at a village bar,' Tess said airily. 'See you.'

'I'll come,' Dottie jumped up, swallowing a mouthful of coffee.

Tess hurried out to the car, she wanted to get away from the villa before Steve realised she was going. Dottie looked curiously at her as they drove out of the gates.

'Are we on the run?'

Tess grimaced. 'I don't want to see Steve for a while.'

'I'd no idea you and he were . . .' Dottie made vague movements, shrugging.

'We're not,' Tess said, very pink.

'Oh, come off it—I'm not your mother, no need to kid me. Why shouldn't you make it with him if you want to? I'm just so surprised, you seemed to squabble with him all the time, but then that's the way it goes, sometimes, isn't it? The more you fancy each other, the more you quarrel.'

'Antagonism one side of the coin, attraction the other,' Tess thought aloud with derision. 'Textbook stuff—am I really that predictable?'

'I don't know,' Dottie said. 'Are you?'

Tess began to laugh. 'Isn't it funny? I think I am, I suppose that's why they put it in textbooks—because it fits a lot of people. Maybe it explains a lot of divorces, too. You may enjoy making it together, but you can't live together without batting each other over the head with a blunt instrument after a few days.'

'Oh, dear,' Dottie said, sounding worried. 'You aren't going to do that to Steve, are you?' She stared at Tess's profile. 'Or are you afraid he may do that to you?'

'Both could happen,' Tess said with angry amusement.

'They do say that the way we pick our men comes from the sort of childhood we had,' Dottie offered. 'I mean, if your parents fight all the time then you repeat the pattern when you get married.'

'My parents didn't fight, I never heard either of them raise a voice,' Tess said flatly, realising that Dottie was hinting at a troubled childhood.

'Mine argued a lot,' Dottie said, laughing. 'They laughed a lot, too. I think they liked arguing, they had a good marriage.'

Tess turned in to the village, frowning, and parked outside the café bar. There were a few workmen eating their breakfast at the small tables inside; they stared as Dottie and Tess walked in and sat down. '*Qu'est-ce que vous voulez, Mesdemoiselles?*' the woman behind the bar asked, leaning over, and Tess smiled up at her and asked for coffee and croissants.

The coffee was strong, the croissants freshly baked; flaking deliciously as they ate them.

'Franco's a friend of Steve's, isn't he?' Tess asked Dottie, who nodded. 'How long has he known him, did he ever say?'

'Steve interviewed Franco a couple of years ago, I think that's the first time they ever met.'

'Interviewed him for what? A newspaper?'

'I think so, I wasn't really that interested. Didn't Steve tell you he used to be a journalist?'

'He told me—did Franco know that Steve wrote plays?'

'Of course he knows, Steve got him tickets for the first night of the last one. Franco said next time he's in London he's going to take me to dinner at the best Italian restaurant in town.' Dottie finished her coffee, sighing. 'Do you think he'll remember? Holiday romances are always the same; you promise all sorts of things and a week later you've forgotten his name.'

'You won't forget Franco's,' Tess said, paying the bill.

'He may forget mine,' Dottie said gloomily, following her out of the bar. They walked down the street to the shop and found it just opening; the smell of newly baked bread was mouthwatering although they had just eaten croissants.

Ten minutes later they packed a number of paper bags of food into the boot of the car and then drove off. 'Back to the villa?' Dottie asked and Tess shrugged.

'I thought I'd take a short drive first.' She was in no hurry to face Steve again. It was a relief to hear that Franco confirmed Steve's identity; yet if they were old friends wouldn't he be prepared to lie? It didn't necessarily prove that Steve was who he claimed to be—and even if he was a playwright that didn't explain his probing into her family relationships. He could be curious simply because such delicate relationships interested him as a writer, of course, but Tess's female intuition warned her that there was far more to it than that.

'Franco suggested we have lunch at Gourdon today,' Dottie reminded her. 'He says the view of the Loup gorge is terrific from there—you can eat at a restaurant looking down a sheer drop to the river.'

'It can be windy up there, though,' Tess said and Dottie made a face.

'Sorry, I forgot you know everywhere around here. Don't you want to come? Franco said he'd pick me up at around noon, but I'd like you and Steve to come too, I think it's more fun going around in a foursome, don't you?'

'I'd love to come,' Tess said, because it was safer in a foursome. She had no intention of being left alone with Steve; especially not at the villa. Anything might happen and her mind veered sharply away from what she meant by that, the pictures she couldn't help conjuring up made her go pink.

'Is that Vence?' Dottie asked, as they approached it from the St Paul district. 'Are there any good shops?'

'There's a cathedral and a pretty square with a fountain in the middle of it,' Tess said. 'Want to see it?'

'I'd like to see the shops,' Dottie said. Her appetite for sight-seeing was strictly limited. 'I want to get some new sandals; I ruined my best pair walking in the sea—those pebbles hurt my feet, I had to put my sandals on.'

They spent some time wandering around the narrow streets of the old town and left around eleven. There was a red car parked outside the villa when they drove in through the gates; Dottie peered excitedly at it. 'Franco must have got here early,' she said, then frowned. 'That isn't the car he had yesterday—he had a Porsche, that's a Renault.'

'Steve must have got his car back at last,' Tess said in dry disbelief, parking just behind it. She hadn't expected his car to re-appear for days; she had even begun to doubt its existence or, at least, to doubt if there was anything wrong with it in the first place. 'Now he can move on, can't he?' she thought to herself as she got out of the car, but did it aloud so that Dottie stared at her in accusing reproach.

'You aren't really going to make him leave now, are you? I thought that you and Steve were . . .'

'We're not,' Tess said very firmly, collecting the shopping bags from the boot. Dottie was unlocking the front door of the villa. 'Hey, take this bag,' Tess called to her. 'I can't manage all this on my own.'

Dottie had begun to turn back when Tess heard her give a loud gasp. 'Tess!' she gulped and Tess swung to stare at the villa. Had a lizard got into the house? Dottie was terrified of them; she was scared of mice and spiders and anything else that crept or crawled or slithered, her atavistic fears were legion and sometimes quite funny.

'What is it now?' Tess asked, smiling, and ready to shoo out of the house whatever had got into it, then her face froze in shock as she saw what had startled Dottie.

Her mother was walking out of the kitchen.

CHAPTER SEVEN

TESS dropped the shopping into Dottie's arms and ran to meet her mother in the middle of the hall. 'What on earth are you doing here?' She hugged Ellen, kissed her cheek and got a firm hug back, as she gabbled, 'Is anything wrong? Why have you come? Are you alone?'

'Calm down, Tess, nothing to get into a panic about.' Ellen's face and voice were as tranquil as ever—she had always been a quietly assured woman who seemed to have no regrets or worries, in spite of the sensitivity of her fine-boned features. Whenever Tess looked at her mother she felt she might well be looking at herself in thirty years time—they had the same slight figure, the same bone structure, the same colouring. Ellen's dark hair was silvered and her throat had the texture of soft crêpe, she had lines of laughter and contentment at eyes and mouth, but even a stranger could see the resemblance at a first glance.

'Why didn't you let me know you were coming?'

'There wasn't time—I must persuade Hal to get a 'phone put into the villa, it's ridiculous not to be able to get in touch when you or Hal are over here. If I'd sent a cable it wouldn't have arrived before I did.'

Dottie had gone into the kitchen to deposit the shopping while they were talking. She came out and gave Ellen a friendly smile. 'Hallo, Mrs Linden, how are you?'

'Hallo, Dottie,' Ellen said. 'I'm fine. How are you? You look as if you're getting a nice tan.'

'Oh, I am—we're having a marvellous holiday. It was very good of your son to lend us this place, it's a beautiful house, I love it here.'

'I'm not too fond of the South of France myself,' Ellen said, glancing around the cool hall. 'I don't like the heat, it saps your energy.'

'I know what you mean,' Dottie said, signalling queried uncertainty to Tess, behind Ellen's back, jerking her head back towards the kitchen and raising her brows. 'Why don't I make you some coffee?' she offered politely, catching Ellen's eye and immediately looking blank. 'Or would you rather have tea?'

'I was just about to do that—thank you, Dottie,' Ellen said. 'I want to have a few words with Tess alone, we'll go into the sitting-room. Just give us five minutes, would you? And make it tea, not coffee—I'm parched!'

'Of course,' Dottie said, nodding vigorously. As Ellen began to walk away, Dottie hissed to Tess, 'Where's Steve? Does she know he's here?'

Tess caught the backward look Ellen gave them and smiled wryly. 'I think she does—he may have gone out or perhaps he's in the pool?'

'Is that your mother's car—or his?' Dottie wondered.

'I'll ask her. If Steve turns up, keep him out of

the sitting-room until I've finished talking to my mother, would you?'

'Sure. I'll be discretion itself,' Dottie said and winked. 'But you're a big girl now, she won't be shocked.'

'I didn't mean that,' Tess said but didn't see the point of explaining what she had meant. She followed her mother into the sitting-room, closing the glass door behind her. Ellen was sitting on the white couch, her small feet curled up under her and her arms clasping her knees; she looked like a child with curious silvery hair, her blue eyes very bright and steady.

Tess sat down on the carpet, her chin on her knees, facing Ellen a few feet away from her. 'Are you here because of the message I left on Johnny's answering machine?' she asked in a frontal attack that made her mother laugh.

'Straight to the point, as always—yes, he rang me as soon as he heard it. It threw him into a panic, he was incoherent at first, I couldn't make head nor tail of what was worrying him.' Her mouth had a tender curve; it often did when she talked about Johnny, and Tess stared at her with baffled uncertainty. Her parents were an enigma to her—she didn't understand them or their relationship.

'I gather he didn't tell Steve Houghton he could borrow the villa?' Tess said flatly, unsurprised by that at least.

'It's more complicated than that,' Ellen said quietly. 'You know that Johnny played in Steve's first hit . . .'

'*Dumb Treason*,' Tess nodded. 'Yes, I know.'

'Johnny told Steve then that he could always borrow the villa, you know the casual way he has . . .'

'With other people's property!' Tess said with scathing irony.

'That isn't fair, Tess, your father helped Hal buy the villa. It was always understood that Johnny and his friends could use it if it was free.' Ellen's voice was stern and Tess made a wry face.

'Okay, I'm sorry, I know Hal lets Johnny use the place whenever he likes.'

'Well, that's how Steve Houghton knew about the villa, but Johnny certainly didn't give him the key.' Ellen paused. 'He had no idea Steve was here until he got your message.'

'I suspected as much,' Tess said rather flatly, frowning. 'Hal keeps a key hidden in the garden shed—I think that's where Steve got it from.'

'No,' Ellen said. 'He got it from an actress who was staying here a couple of months ago. She had a key and didn't give it back to Johnny.'

Tess stiffened, watching her mother. 'An actress?' She didn't need to ask if the unidentified actress had had a relationship with Johnny; she could read the fact in her mother's calm face. How could Ellen look so tranquil?

'She was in *Dumb Treason*—Anna Cadogan, a tall girl with a remarkable voice,' Ellen said with the fair-mindedness that sometimes made Tess want to scream at her. 'Very beautiful girl, you must remember her, she played the secretary.'

'I remember her,' Tess said, frowning as she

remembered something else—Anna had been the name someone had mentioned to Steve at the Eden-Roc. 'This girl lent the key to Steve?'

'Johnny thinks so.'

'He hasn't asked her?'

'He hadn't managed to get hold of her when he rang me—she's away visiting a relative.' Ellen paused as Dottie tapped on the door and then came into the room carrying a tea tray. 'Oh, thank you, Dottie, put it on the table, will you?'

'I brought you some rolls and jam in case you're hungry—or there are some biscuits.' Dottie carefully put the tray down and smiled at Mrs Linden. 'Shall I pour it for you?'

Tess uncoiled and stood up. 'No, I'll do it, Dottie.'

'Okay.' Dottie discreetly removed herself, closing the door behind her, and Ellen looked after her, smiling.

'She's a nice girl.'

'Very,' Tess said, pouring the tea with a hand that shook slightly. 'What's the connection between Steve Houghton and this Anna Cadogan? She's an old flame of his, I suppose?' Steve had tacitly admitted as much, although he hadn't hinted at Johnny's involvement with the girl. Was Johnny's affair with her over? Not all Johnny's discarded lady friends were amiably disposed towards him after he had dropped them although, for some inexplicable reason, many of them did remain his friends. What magic did he use? How did he persuade women to forgive him after he had callously ended an affair? Tess had

asked herself that question a hundred times
before without getting any glimmer of an
answer—if her father had magical charm she had
never been touched by it.

'Oh, dear,' Ellen said on a sigh, accepting her cup
of tea. 'I gather Steve *was* in love with her, he knew
her before the play opened. It was Steve who
suggested her name for the part, she was quite a
newcomer and there was some trouble over
auditioning her at all. Johnny wanted someone
else, but in the end Steve got his way and she was
really very good. She made a big hit in the part.'

'Not least with Johnny,' murmured Tess
angrily, sitting down with her own tea. 'I see the
picture. Johnny rang you in a panic and you came
all this way just to tell me Steve Houghton had
no right to be here—you could have sent a
telegram, but you didn't. You flew here at once
which means there's something very serious
behind all this, and it doesn't take Einstein to
figure out what's going on!'

Ellen glanced at her wryly. 'Don't work
yourself up into one of your tempers!'

'I'm not bad tempered!'

'Not bad tempered—just hot tempered,' Ellen
said. 'I came because Johnny was over-reacting—
he's in the middle of making a T.V. play and
couldn't get away himself. I didn't want him
getting into a state so I said I'd come and sort it
all out. You know what a child he is.'

'A child?' Tess said with disbelief and her
mother laughed, her eyes full of warmth, as
though Tess amused her.

'Oh, he is, Tess—a spoilt child, without any adult inhibitions or controls—he can't help being the way he is; it's all part of his amazing gift. He gives himself to whatever he's doing with a hundred per cent of his energy but he burns out quickly—his attention span is limited by the sheer power he gives things. That's why he hates long runs, he can't keep his interest and once he's bored he loses power. He gets bored easily.'

'With women, too,' Tess said shortly.

'Of course,' her mother said, watching her and sighing again. 'You can't expect a man like Johnny to be like other people, in many ways he's hopelessly blind about real feelings. On stage he instinctively understands emotion—but off stage he doesn't have a clue. He's a blundering, well-meaning child—in some ways he's whatever part he is playing at the time, that's why he falls in love with people all the time. It isn't real, it just spills over from the play he's·in with them, haven't you realised that it's always the actress playing opposite him?'

Tess frowned, thinking back over the years—was that true? Faces and names flashed in front of her eyes as she remembered a whole string of women and with a stab of surprise realised that her mother had been right. It had never dawned on her before.

Slowly she said, 'He's just acting every time? With all of them?'

'And quite often they're just acting, too,' Ellen said with calm humour. 'If they're going to give themselves to a part it means that for several hours each night they aren't aware of anything outside the play and it's very hard to step back into ordinary life when the curtain goes down. The whole cast gets so close, they feel they know each other intimately. It's an illusion, of course, and when a run ends they may never see each other again but for that little time it seems totally real to them.'

'Are you trying to tell me that none of his affairs has meant a thing?' Tess asked incredulously.

'One or two may have been serious,' Ellen said cheerfully. 'The others were all a game. He likes falling in love with someone new—it makes him feel young again. He loves the rituals of being in love—sending flowers, having private little suppers after a show, having secrets. He's hooked on the kick he gets from all that.'

'Mother, how can you talk about it? How can you take it so lightly? Doesn't it hurt your feelings at *all*?'

Ellen looked at her drily. 'It upsets you far more than it upsets me. I love your father dearly, I'm proud of him, he's a great man, in his way— but I'm not jealous of the others because I'm not in love with him. I haven't been for years. You can't be in love with a man you see so clearly; there's no mystery for me and love is half mystery, the discovery that the other person is different, is separate and mysterious. Johnny's more my child than my lover now, he has been for years. He needs me to mother him, that's why he always comes running back—I'm his safety net, his security blanket.'

Tess put her empty cup down on the table. 'And that satisfies you? That sort of marriage?' she asked in a voice she tried to make expressionless. She didn't fool her mother, Ellen was smiling as she looked at her.

'Tess, I'm not highly sexed and I don't like life to be too exciting. I wanted exactly the sort of life I've had—peaceful and happy, with my home and garden and children, and Hal's brood whenever he brings them over, and my cats. What more could I ask for? I'm too old to be jealous over Johnny's little escapades.'

'It sounds so sad,' Tess said, and Ellen shook her head, laughing.

'That's because you're a romantic—you think that's all there is to life, being in love.'

'Oh, don't be ridiculous, Mother, I've never thought anything of the kind!' Tess said indignantly, flushing. 'Anyway,' she added hurriedly, changing the subject, 'what has all this to do with Steve being here? Why did he come? What is he up to?'

'He's writing a biography of Johnny,' Ellen said and Tess gasped.

'Oh!'

Ellen's face was wry. 'Yes, I'm afraid so! When a publisher approached Johnny and said the firm would like to do a biography, Johnny was thrilled, of course, and he suggested Steve should write it. Steve had done one other book—on famous actors of the Victorian era. Johnny handed over to Steve all his letters, diaries, programmes—his private souvenirs—and he gave

Steve permission to talk to anyone who would talk to him.' Ellen made a little grimace. 'And then everything changed . . .'

Tess had already guessed. 'Then he took up with Anna Cadogan and suddenly Steve didn't like Johnny any more?'

'Exactly,' Ellen sighed. 'The affair with Anna was over inside a few months, that's the stupid part of it—it flared up, burnt like a forest fire for weeks at a time and then died down.' Catching her daughter's angry stare, Ellen said flatly: 'On both sides, Tess—I've seen Anna recently, she isn't bitter over Johnny, she's rather funny about him, actually. I like her; she has style. She could laugh the whole thing off.'

'But Steve couldn't?' Tess said in cold, tight tones.

'Apparently not,' Ellen said with regret. 'Poor Steve got badly hurt, I'm afraid.'

Tess swallowed, her throat hot with jealousy and pain. She fought to keep both feelings out of her face.

'And he's writing a biography of Johnny,' she thought aloud in a voice she only just kept steady. 'Which gives him the perfect opportunity of cutting Johnny into tiny little pieces in public.'

Ellen looked at her wryly. 'And your father is kicking himself because it was his idea to get Steve to do that book!'

'Couldn't Johnny withdraw his consent to the biography?'

'A little too late to do that; Steve has a contract with the publisher, they've paid him an advance and, anyway, Johnny doesn't actually know what Steve intends to do, he's only guessing.'

'Pretty accurately, I'd say,' Tess muttered, remembering the constant needle of Steve's questions about her father, his attempts to get her to tell him how she really felt about Johnny. 'It will be a literary assassination,' she said and Ellen looked disturbed.

'You think Johnny is right to be worried, then? Steve does have a tough face.'

'Ruthless,' Tess said with terse bitterness. He hadn't had a qualm about using her to get at her father, he had even been prepared to make love to her to do it.

'What frightens your father is the way Steve has turned up here,' Ellen said, watching her questioningly. 'The press has always run stories about Johnny's private life, he doesn't mind that. What worries him is that Steve might try to pump you and write about how you see Johnny. Your father knows you're not exactly a fan of his.'

Tess gave a grim little smile. 'And he was afraid I'd give Steve weapons to use against him? I'm a little more loyal than that.'

'I told your father he didn't have to worry about you,' Ellen said gently. 'You've always tried not to say a word against him, even to me. I appreciate that, Tess, I know you've often been critical of my attitude and maybe I should have talked to you frankly a long time ago, but I'm not the type who likes discussing such private matters, even with my daughter. I was sure that you wouldn't discuss your father with an outsider.'

Tess flushed to the hairline. 'The trouble is . . .' she began and her mother looked sharply at her.

'Yes?'

'He's been here for a few days now and he kept asking me questions; of course, I suspected, I said as little as possible, but he may have picked up all sorts of clues.' Tess was cold with anger as she remembered the tactics Steve had used to get her to talk about her father. 'He's unscrupulous in his methods,' she muttered, looking away from Ellen's probing eyes. 'I know he kept notes of what I said . . .' She told her mother about Steve's leather-bound notebook and the short-hand which filled it. 'I don't remember saying anything much, but one evening I was almost drunk,' she said with bitterness. 'God knows what he got out of me then.'

'It's my fault,' Ellen said and Tess wailed.

'Oh, Mother! How can you say that?'

'I mean it—I should have taken you into my confidence long ago, I shouldn't have let you go on blaming your father when really he isn't the sort of man you think. I tried to show you how it was without having to say anything.'

'But I'm as insensitive as Johnny,' Tess said with grim humour. 'You did show me but I didn't see; I have to see facts written down in black and white, I could kick myself.' She was thinking hard and hating what she was realising. Steve had been angry with her father over Anna

Cadogan—he must have been deeply in love with her. Johnny's affair with her had left Steve bitter and vindictive—his proposed biography had become a weapon to use against Johnny and he had somehow known that Tess was here at the villa. Perhaps Johnny had mentioned it to Anna Cadogan and she had told Steve? Steve had come here deliberately, to get her to talk about her father, and maybe he had known before he came how much she hated her father? Johnny might have mentioned something of it to him long ago, or else Steve had simply picked up the fact when he visited the family home and met Ellen. Steve was quick-witted and shrewd; he didn't need facts written down in black and white, he picked up such clues without needing further evidence than a look, a word, a silence.

'He's despicable,' she said aloud, her throat full of bitterness and the taste of deceit. Steve had tried to get to her simply in order to make her confide in him.

'Are all men so self-centred and two-faced?' she asked and her mother looked at her anxiously, frowning. 'Ready to use people, talk them into caring, lie and cheat and then walk away without giving a damn?'

'Tess, what has been going on here?' Ellen asked, perturbed.

'You may not care whether Johnny has affairs or not—but what damage has he done to others? What did he do to Anna Cadogan? You don't know, do you? You say she's tolerant and it didn't mean a thing to her—but how do *you* know? Don't tell me that all the women Johnny has been involved with have been happy at the end of the affair; some have got hurt, they must have been, and there have been so many. They can't all have been as frivolous as Johnny is, or as cold-hearted.'

'No, you can't call him that,' Ellen protested. 'He's . . .'

'Egocentric, childish, selfish, greedy,' Tess said fiercely. 'You've told me so yourself—he's a child, you said. He can't discipline himself, you said. He has no real feelings, you said—he doesn't know the meaning of the word love. It's all acting, with him.'

'Is this how you've been talking to Steve Houghton? Is this what he's going to put in that book?' Ellen stood up, very pale, and Tess faced her aggressively.

'At least I haven't lied to him—at least whatever I've said has been the truth. I do know what real feelings are. I'm not a child. I'm not self-centred or cold. I'm a human being and I have blood in my veins. I'm not a mere shadow, like my father.'

Ellen turned towards the door, her body stiff as she walked. 'Where is Steve Houghton?'

'I don't know,' Tess said. 'And I don't care.' She was looking at her mother with remote eyes and Ellen looked back at her with a mixture of bewilderment and distress.

'Your idea of a marriage baffles me,' Tess said. 'I used to hate my father because I thought he'd made you unhappy. I was sorry for you. Isn't that silly? But I was stupid not to realise that neither of you wasted much emotion on anything. You weren't unhappy. You had a cosy life, with everything you needed, and you watched Johnny having affair after affair without turning a hair because you didn't care. Maybe it was because you didn't care that Johnny had all those affairs. God knows. I hope I never turn into a semi-detached woman like you. I nearly did, you know. I came pretty close to it, just trying not to get hurt, refusing to care in case I was let down. And that's exactly the road to take if you want to end up with your feelings in deep freeze and your life as neat and clean and empty as a sterilised milk bottle.'

'Tess!' Ellen was distraught. 'You aren't being fair!'

Tess laughed shortly. 'This isn't a court of law. I'm not a judge. I'm just saying it how I see it.'

'You're upset, I know that—but you shouldn't take things so intensely. You worry me.' Ellen's voice was soothing, she looked distinctly anxious.

'Oh, don't let me do that, Mother,' Tess said with tired irony. 'Don't break the habit of a lifetime and start caring about something. Who knows what might come of it?'

She went out of the room, leaving her mother behind, wishing she could leave the villa altogether and be alone for days on end to absorb all the new ideas she had been given over the past hour. She had to stay, though; she had to face Steve, find out exactly what he meant to write in his biography of her father and challenge his right to publish anything she had said to him.

Where was he, anyway? She checked in the pool, but it was empty, the blue water glimmering under the sunlight. The trees rustled, their shadows moving in flickering black and white on the path, while she watched, like someone at a grainy old silent film, a real three-hankie weepie, where emotions were larger than life and people mimed grief in huge, sweeping gestures you couldn't fail to understand. It must have been nice to live in a time when emotion was so simple, and life's edges hadn't blurred together so that you no longer knew where you were or what you felt.

Oh, but her own emotional instincts had been right on target as far as Steve was concerned. Her intuition had been infallible—Steve *had* been lying to her, using her, cynically manipulating her.

Ellen's complacency, her tranquil self-protection, her emotional isolation, offended Tess deeply, yet she reluctantly saw why her mother had retreated to that halcyon corner far from any chance of getting hurt. Ellen was a burnt-out case; she might once have been ravaged by the disease but love was no threat to her any more.

Tess felt oddly scared as she thought about it. She didn't want to find herself on some emotional desert island; surely life offered more than that? Wasn't there a safe course between the two extremes? She didn't have to pick a man like Johnny—or Steve, she angrily admitted to herself. Yes, that was just it—Steve did have qualities in common with her father. He was ruthless, opportunist, ego-centred and ready to use emotional weapons to get what he wanted from the women he met.

Had he been deeply in love with Anna Cadogan? A cold splinter of pain was lodged in her heart. She turned and walked back to the villa, biting her lip. She wouldn't think about it. Damn him; how could he have come here, cold-bloodedly, intending to seduce her into giving him the ammunition to use on her father? That was what he had done. She had sensed it somehow right from the start—and now she knew she had been right, her suspicions completely justified, and she wished to God she had been totally wrong.

As she turned the corner on to the drive she saw Steve getting out of a long, white Jaguar, the fast XJS model with the sleek elongated bonnet. He waited as he saw her, his face shuttered and remote, lids drooping across his eyes.

'I got my car back, as you see,' he drawled.

She felt feverish and shaky with rage. She wanted to hit him. 'Then you can hit the road, now, can't you?' she said and was amazed by the sound of her own voice. It sounded high, unstable, frenetic. 'And before you get out of here I've just got one thing to say to you—if you print a single solitary word I've said to you, in this biography of my father, I'll bring a law suit! I'll sue you for every penny you've got!'

His mouth was hard. He didn't seem surprised—yet he couldn't know that her mother had arrived, could he?

'So you know about that! Is he here?' He looked towards the villa and Tess felt even angrier as she saw his mouth twist.

'No, he isn't, but my mother is—and *she* doesn't want you around either. So you can go upstairs and pack, then go.'

'He sent your mother,' Steve said with bitter derision. 'He didn't even have the nerve to come himself. I might have expected it.'

'He's working, he can't get away.' Why am I defending Johnny? Tess asked herself and the only answer was that he was still her father, whatever he had done. Ellen was right—he was a great man and someone to be proud of, you couldn't simply judge him by ordinary standards and forget the rest of his extraordinary career. Johnny wasn't just an unforgettably beautiful man, he was an actor of tremendous power, he lived at a different pace from everyone around him.

Steve laughed, his eyes unhooded now and brilliant with anger.

'I'm proud of him,' Tess said with a shock of discovery, hurling the words at Steve but amazing herself far more.

'You're proud of his tom-cat love life, are you?' Steve asked, obviously expecting to catch her on the raw, but Tess looked at him with fierce contempt.

'He's my father. I love him.' It was the first time she had thought it, let alone said it, and she was high on the shocks she was giving herself.

'He's a great actor. You have no right to despise him.'

'*You* do!' Steve said, staring as if he didn't recognise her any more—and she wasn't surprised, because she didn't know herself, she never had, she was only just beginning to understand anything about herself. 'You've admitted it to me; you know what sort of man he is and you detest him.'

'You aren't using me to knife my father in the back! Whatever I may think of him, I think a damned sight less of you.' She saw the leap of surprise in his eyes and swept on angrily. 'The methods you used to get me to talk about him were as low as you could get.'

His face was dark red now and his eyes were confused. 'All right, I lied to you—he didn't actually know I was at the villa, but he had said I could borrow it any time I wished.'

'That wasn't what I meant—and you know it.'

Their eyes tangled and Steve's face tightened; she saw the sharp angle of the bones under his smooth brown skin, the tension of mouth and jaw.

'Tess, it wasn't all lies,' he said huskily, taking a step towards her, his hand reaching for her.

She slapped him away, stepping back. 'I know about Anna Cadogan!' She flung at him fiercely. 'So don't lie any more, you'll just be wasting your time! If I didn't despise you, I'd feel sorry for you, because if she had ever cared twopence for you she wouldn't have looked twice at Johnny. If you want to be angry with anyone, be angry with yourself for caring about someone who didn't love *you*.' Her voice had taken on a jagged edge, it shook, and she bit her inner lip to steady it. She wasn't going to cry, she wouldn't give him the satisfaction.

'Who told you?' he asked flatly, looking rather taken aback. 'Your *mother*?' That seemed to amaze him; did he think Ellen didn't know Johnny like the back of her hand?

'I notice you don't deny that that's your real motive for wanting to attack my father,' she said. 'You tried to seduce me into telling you what you wanted to know. You have no right to despise Johnny—he may be egocentric but at least he isn't vindictive.'

'Neither am I!'

'What else do you call it? Johnny took your woman and you wanted to hit back so you came here deliberately to use me to hurt him. You knew I was at the villa, didn't you? She told you, I suppose?'

'Anna mentioned it,' he admitted and she ground her teeth together at the way he said the other woman's name. So this was how jealousy felt? Her stomach lurched in sick rejection and her throat was dry with tension. 'You're making it too simple, Tess. I wasn't out for blood. I wasn't looking for revenge. I wanted to write about the real man; warts and all—it was time the public image was pulled down and the real Johnny Linden was on show.'

She looked at him disbelievingly. 'Do you seriously expect me to believe that garbage?'

'Look, I was very angry when Anna dropped me for him—I admit that.'

'How honest of you!' she mocked bitterly, and he visibly seethed with impatience, his eyes hard and bright.

'But I still intend to do an honest job on this book. I won't write one single word I can't prove to be the truth. You can't quarrel with that, can you?'

Tess smiled with barbed distaste. 'You make it sound so reasonable and irreproachable, don't you? You hate Johnny because he stole your woman but you've rationalised that into something else. You're just kidding yourself when you say you want a warts and all portrait—you want to kill Johnny with a typewriter. Well, I won't help you do it. I don't say there aren't some black spots on Johnny's character—but he's human, everyone has faults, and there's a lot more to him than that. If you show him as some sort of monster, as I suspect you will, you'll be lying just as much as if you painted him as a saint.'

'I've already told you, I'm not going to tell anything but the truth!'

'As you see it!' she added ironically.

'Yes,' he said, then his eyes changed and he grimaced, coming closer again. 'Tess, listen to me . . .'

'Never again,' she said. 'You don't get a second chance, Steve. Stay away from me and keep your hands to yourself.' She stopped speaking abruptly, staring past him, her face startled. 'Now who is that? What is going on today? This place is like a railway station in the rush hour.'

Steve turned and looked down the drive at the open gate where a yellow taxi was just turning to drive towards them. The woman in the back leaned forward at that moment, the sun striking sparks from her long red hair. Tess heard Steve draw a sharp, surprised breath and looked sideways at him in suspicion.

'Who is it?' she asked, expecting the answer he gave a moment later in a flat, quiet voice.

'It's Anna.'

CHAPTER EIGHT

'WHAT is she doing here?' Tess asked, tension in every muscle of her body making her feel as if she was on the rack. Was Anna Cadogan in some sort of conspiracy with Steve? Was that why she had given him the key to the villa? Tess looked at him angrily and then stared at the other woman who had got out of the taxi and was paying the driver. It was blindingly obvious now that Steve had had inside information; he had known that Tess would be here, he had known she didn't have much love for her father. He had got all that from Anna Cadogan, but now that Johnny knew what was going on there was no point in hiding Anna's part in the plot so she had come here to join her fellow conspirator. But was that all Steve was to her? Were they lovers again?

'I'm sure you can guess,' Steve said with biting hostility and Tess felt all the colour draining from her face at his tone. He had spoken as if he hated her, she flinched at the thought. Did he hate her? He had been pretending to find her attractive, he had made love to her—but now that his conspiracy had been discovered he wasn't bothering to pretend any more, especially now that his real love had arrived.

'I suppose I can,' she said in a thin, tight voice.

Steve turned his head and looked at her harshly, the bones of his face locked in rage.

'You know why she's here, as well as I do!'

'Oh, not as well as *you* do,' Tess said with bitterness. 'I only suspect why she's here—you know! Come to make sure you don't get too involved with me, has she? How flattering. But I don't think she's actually seen me, she probably thinks I look like Johnny—and if I did maybe she would have cause for jealousy.'

Steve stared at her, his face blank.

'Well, go and set her mind at rest,' Tess told him sharply. 'I don't want her in the villa, I don't want her anywhere near me. Take her to the Eden-Roc—that's where you usually stay when you're in the South of France, isn't it? Oh, yes, I guessed that, too. You didn't fool me for an instant, even if you thought you did. I was on to you from the first day.'

'*Were* you?' he said oddly.

'You'd better believe it.' Tess turned towards the villa and flung over her shoulder, 'And don't come back, with or without her. Franco can pack up your clothes and bring them back with him tonight. I don't want to see your face again.'

She heard Anna Cadogan's deep, smoky voice before she slammed the front door of the villa. 'Steve, darling . . .'

Tess ran upstairs, biting down hard on her inner lip, refusing to release the tears burning under her lids. In her own room she stood for a few minutes, fighting with those tears until her anger had won and driven the pain underground.

She washed her face in stingingly cold water. It helped; she felt able to go back to face her mother once she had put on fresh make-up and brushed her hair, able to smile and look calm without giving any sign that there was a cold stone where her heart had been and her veins were running with ice-water instead of blood. Steve had made a fool of her, in spite of her suspicion; he had got to her through all her carefully erected defences. She hated herself. She hated Steve far more.

As she came down the stairs Dottie opened the front door, saying, 'Hallo, I wondered where you'd got to!' to a male shape outside.

Tess was about to tell her not to let Steve back into the house when she realised that it was Franco arriving to take them to Gourdon. He was alone. Squinting through the open door Tess saw no sign of Steve or Anna Cadogan and the white Jag had gone. She told herself she was delighted, but contrarily felt like biting someone, which may have showed in her face, her over-bright eyes and clenched teeth, because both Franco and Dottie looked at her uneasily.

'*Ciao!*' Franco said, keeping a safe distance. 'Is a lovely day for driving to Gourdon, no wind, very sunny. Steve around?'

'No,' Tess said.

'I thought I saw him talking to you a few minutes ago,' Dottie said with hesitation, and when Tess glared at her, furious at the thought of Dottie watching her with Steve, Dottie hurriedly said: 'But maybe I didn't.'

'Oh, don't be ridiculous,' Tess snapped. 'Of

course you did, he was here, but now he's probably driving his girlfriend to the Eden-Roc.' She didn't want Dottie lying to placate her, she wasn't a fretful child and didn't want to be treated like one.

'Girlfriend?' repeated Franco, looking baffled.

'Anna Cadogan,' Tess said with distaste.

'Anna?' Franco obviously knew her. He ran a hand over his immaculate black hair, straightened his immaculate blue silk tie, his automatic gestures giving him time to get over his amazement, not to mention alarm. 'Oh, Anna, sure,' he said, eyeing Tess uneasily.

Obviously Dottie hadn't been watching Tess and Steve long enough, she had no idea who Anna Cadogan was, her jaw had dropped and her eyes glazed. 'Girlfriend?' she repeated, however, latching on to the important point. 'His girlfriend arrived?' She stared at Tess with consternation. 'Oh. Oh, Tess!'

Tess did not want to be sympathised with or wept over. She froze into stiff indifference, her eyes silently repelling Dottie's dismay.

'She came to join him at the villa?' Franco enquired and Dottie made a furious noise.

'You were right about him first off, Tess,' she said. 'You were absolutely spot on. A rat, you said, the minute you saw him, but I wouldn't believe you. He never breathed a word about her, did he?'

'You don't know about Anna?' Franco asked, still trying to discover how much they now knew. Tess eyed him thoughtfully; how much did

Franco know, that was the question, and how much could she and Dottie get out of him?

Franco met her gaze and began to look distinctly unhappy; he backed to the door, saying they ought to be getting on to Gourdon. 'We are late for lunch, it will be ruined!' He held out a hand to Dottie imploringly. 'You come now, Dottie?'

Dottie looked at Tess, a question in her eyes.

'You know the real reason why Steve is here, don't you, Franco?' Tess said softly. 'He told you that he wanted to trick me into talking about my father, that's why you were to whisk Dottie away and leave me alone with Steve.'

Dottie's mouth opened but no sound came out. Franco looked anxiously at her, shaking his head. 'Is not like that,' he said, and then, his English deserting him, jabbered in hurried Italian for a moment.

Dottie descended on him in a flurry of small fists and kicking feet and Franco backed, his hands up in front of his face. 'Oh, no, Dottie, please! You don't believe . . .' He suddenly put his hands down and grabbed her shoulders, pinioning her arms to her sides. Dottie kicked his ankle. Hopping on one leg, Franco said: '*Cara*, no, no. Okay, I tell you. Honestly, cara, this is how it is . . . Steve ring me, say I got two lovely girls coming to lunch at the Eden-Roc, one for you, one for me? He says that it is the dark little one he likes—I get the other. Well, I don't see you, Dottie, but I say okay—but when I see you I am very happy with the arrangement.'

Dottie kicked his ankle again. 'That's to teach you not to lie to me,' she said through her teeth. 'You promised me you'd never lie to me.'

'And you believed him?' Tess asked drily.

'I'm an idiot,' Dottie agreed.

'Oh, no,' Franco said earnestly, kissing her ear as Dottie quickly turned her head to avoid letting his mouth touch hers. 'I'm crazy about you!' he said to her profile.

'Are you married?' Dottie asked suspiciously.

'No, I swear it—on my mother's grave.'

'Is your mother dead?' Dottie demanded and Franco looked confused.

'No, she lives in Rome, but you know—is an expression. I'm not married, Dottie. I give you my word of honour.'

'Hah!' Dottie said.

'You don't laugh at my honour,' Franco said, suddenly very Italian; his black eyes intense and insulted. 'No, Dottie, when I say that—every word is the solemn truth!'

'Rat!' Dottie said.

'I can't tell you the truth because Steve ask me not to and Steve is my friend,' Franco announced, still in his Roman mood, dignity pervading every line of him.

'Has Anna been staying at the Eden-Roc?' asked Tess.

'No. I haven't seen her, anyway.' Franco held Dottie with one arm while his other hand stroked her long, richly coloured hair, soothing her. 'Steve didn't tell me she was coming.'

'Is she in on Steve's conspiracy?' Tess

demanded and Franco looked blank.

'What conspiracy? I don't know what you're talking about. There's no conspiracy. Steve had a fling with Anna a long time ago—you know, last year, sometime.'

'Oh, centuries ago,' Dottie said bitterly, tearing herself out of his arms. 'Boy, you have a weird idea of time.'

'My English isn't so hot,' Franco said pleadingly. 'You know that, Dottie.'

'I never want to see you again,' Dottie told him.

'No, listen—this Steve and Anna thing—that's over. Steve told me so and anyway, when I see him with Tess it's obvious he likes her a lot, they're always laughing, having fun together, is very nice.' Franco smiled at Tess with imploring eyes. 'I don't understand why Anna has come but you shouldn't worry, Tess. He really goes for you.'

'Now hop it,' Dottie said, opening the door.

'*Cara*,' Franco begged, trying to get her back into his arms.

'I'm going to find my mother,' Tess said, leaving them to it, and retreating into the kitchen where she found Ellen contemplating the contents of the larder.

'I feel like paella,' Ellen said. 'There's a tin of shrimps and some anchovies and that cold chicken in the fridge and the garlic sausage—that should make a very good paella.'

'Did you see Anna Cadogan drive up?' Tess asked and Ellen nodded casually.

Tess felt self-conscious after the things she had said to Ellen not long ago but her mother's manner was as calm as ever. The emotional scene earlier might never have happened. Tess didn't make the mistake of apologising; she knew that Ellen was establishing their relationship on the old pattern, that was the way Ellen wanted it and Tess accepted it wordlessly. In a sense, that was apology enough. She loved her mother, she made no attempt to come any closer, she knew she never would again. Love was a sort of resignation, sometimes; that was the way Ellen was, you loved her that way or you didn't love her at all.

'Anna Cadogan must have been in on Steve's conspiracy,' Tess said.

'Or Johnny managed to get in touch with her and she came here for the same reason I did,' Ellen said. 'That seems far more likely to me. Anna's not the vindictive type.'

'She told Steve I was here and she lent him the key!'

'She may not have realised what he meant to do,' said Ellen. 'How many of us will be here for lunch?'

'I'm not sure, hang on,' Tess said and opened the door to check how Dottie and Franco were getting on. They were kissing passionately so Tess shut the door again.

'Look, why don't we go out for lunch? You don't want to cook while you're in France. We'll go to Nice and find a fabulous restaurant, shall we?'

'Nice is hectic,' Ellen said, wrinkling her nose. 'Worse than London.'

'Vence?'

'Do you know a good restaurant there?'

'Several—cosy little family places with no frills and terrific food.' Tess knew the sort of restaurant her mother liked; Ellen laughed.

Dottie sidled into the kitchen, flushed and bright-eyed, giving Tess a sheepish smile. 'We're going to Gourdon—are you and Mrs Linden coming? We'd love to have you.'

'No, thank you, Dottie—we'd just decided to eat at Vence so that my mother can do some shopping after lunch.'

'Enjoy your drive,' Ellen said.

Dottie looked at the assembled tins and packages on the kitchen table and Ellen told her she meant to make paella.

'For supper tonight, why don't you ask Franco to join us?'

'Okay, thank you,' Dottie said delightedly. 'See you later, then, we'll be back around seven—is that all right with you?'

'Feel free,' Tess said, smiling at her. 'We'll eat around eight to give you plenty of time to make your way back here. Make sure Franco drives carefully on those hairpin bends—the road to Gourdon is a nightmare. Tell Franco that I'd be grateful if he'd pack up Steve Houghton's things and take the case back to the Eden-Roc with him when he goes tonight. I don't want Steve to have any excuse for showing up here again.'

Dottie looked at her with sympathy, nodding. 'I'll tell Franco.'

When she had gone Ellen asked sharply, 'Has Steve left? I thought he was outside with Anna. I saw them talking on the drive, I expected her to come in to the villa.'

'I told Steve to go and take her with him.' Tess tried to sound cool and off hand and only succeeded in sounding like someone trying not to cry, and that made her angry. She compressed her lips together to stop them trembling and looked at her watch to give herself something else to do. 'It's nearly one o'clock—we'd better go and have this lunch before we're too late to get in anywhere.'

'Why don't we just have a salad here?' Ellen asked. 'I'd rather stay at the villa, really, it's less trouble to make a meal than to go out. I've been travelling for hours and I'm tired, Tess.'

'I'm sorry, I should have thought of that,' Tess said. 'Of course we'll stay here, sorry to have been thoughtless.'

'Don't be silly,' Ellen soothed, giving her a wry look. 'You take everything too seriously, Tess, you always did, even as a baby—big, solemn eyes and straight black hair that was always in a tangle because you would grab at it with your sticky little fingers. You were such a serious baby—Hal was quite different, he took life much more easily.' She cleared the table as she talked and produced some tins of sardines which she opened while Tess was making a salad.

'You were always your father's favourite, he

wanted to call you Ophelia but I put my foot down on that—I wasn't having a child of mine saddled with a name like Ophelia.'

'Thank God,' Tess said with fervour, and Ellen laughed.

'I'd let Johnny have his way with Hal—he'd just played in *Henry IV* and was rehearsing *Henry V*—he was determined to call his son Hal and I quite like the name. It doesn't sound too theatrical. But Ophelia was too much.'

'Much too much,' Tess said, tossing the salad. 'Mind you, I never liked *Tess of the d'Urbervilles*. Too depressing.'

'Oh, but realistic,' said Ellen. 'Hardy knew the truth about life.'

Tess turned to stare at her, struck by a sudden glimpse inside her mother's head; her fatalism and calm resignation. Ellen expected life to offer little but quiet duty and a familiar round of days, that was why she read Hardy all the time, he had a similar mind, he didn't expect much, either.

'Mayonnaise or lemon and vinegar dressing?' she asked Ellen wryly.

'Oh, the lemon and vinegar will be fine,' Ellen said, watching her mix it and pour it over the tossed salad, before tossing lightly once more. 'This looks delicious—shall we eat in the hall? I'll take the sardines and the cheese through and lay the table.'

They had almost finished their lunch when they heard the sound of tyres screeching on the drive and then the slam of a car door. Tess was on her feet a second too late; Steve opened the front door of the villa as she shot towards it to stop him coming inside.

'Get out,' she said ferociously, her blue eyes spitting fire at him, leaping to block his entry.

'Don't be stupid, Tess,' he said with an impatient, frowning glance. 'I've got to talk to you.'

'There's nothing to talk about, and I don't want to talk to you anyway.'

'Tess!' Ellen said gently and Tess looked back at her, scowling. 'I want to talk to Steve,' her mother told her and Tess fell back from the door without another word. Steve walked past her. Tess looked out of the door; there was no sign of Anna Cadogan and the white car was empty.

'What have you done with her?' she asked Steve furiously. 'Taken her to the Eden-Roc to wait for you?'

'Anna is staying with friends in Monaco—I drove her back there,' Steve said, his voice brusque, then he walked over to offer his hand to Ellen. 'Hallo, Mrs Linden, how are you?'

The pretence of courtesy made Tess want to scream; she compromised by letting the door slam, it let off some steam anyway, but brought her a dark glower from Steve and a rueful shake of the head from Ellen. Tess met both with defiance, her chin up.

'You're looking well, Steve—what a marvellous tan,' said Ellen, and the polite small talk set Tess's teeth on edge. Steve was planning to write a vicious attack on Johnny. Why was her mother smiling at him as if he was an old friend she was delighted to see again?

'I'm fine,' Steve said, and Tess laughed aloud, cynically, which brought her another sideways glare from him. She met it with a sneer, her lip curled.

'Oh, don't worry, he's just fine,' she told her mother with angry mockery. 'He's managed to worm his way in here, lie his head off, get me talking about my father when I was drunk and didn't know what I was saying—so that he can write a book that flays the skin off Johnny. Yes, he's just fine, thank you.'

'Tess, why don't you go and make some coffee while I talk to Steve?' Ellen suggested discreetly, but Tess looked at her with fulminating eyes.

'I want to hear what he says to you. I'm curious to know just how far he'll go to convince you that Johnny doesn't need to worry about this book. Don't believe a word he says; he's a smooth liar.'

'I'm quite capable of deciding for myself whether someone is lying or not,' Ellen said, but she looked at Steve ruefully. 'Tess has a habit of insisting on blunt truth so we might as well admit that I'm here to find out what *you're* doing here, Steve. Johnny was taken aback when he heard you were here—he had no idea.' She paused then added delicately, 'Did he?'

'Why wrap it up?' Tess demanded. 'Johnny hadn't given him the key, Johnny didn't know he was here—but he told me that he had paid Johnny two weeks' rent for the villa when he had done nothing of the kind! That's fraud and if we call in the police he could be arrested for it. Why don't we do that? Dottie and I got back to find him here—he'd let himself in and that's breaking and entering.'

'Sure there's nothing else you could get me for?' Steve asked bitingly. 'Fraud and breaking and entering—surely you could come up with some other charges?'

'Sexual assault?' Tess flung at him. 'Getting a girl drunk and trying to make love to her?'

'Trying?' mocked Steve and her face burned. 'You're horrifying your mother,' he added. 'She'll imagine the worst.' He smiled at Ellen with infuriating charm and Tess could have hit him as her mother smiled back at him, with somewhat uncertain eyes, but still somehow coaxed to smile. 'Take no notice, Mrs Linden— Tess is exaggerating. She may not have inherited her father's talent on the stage but she has a taste for melodrama, all the same, but you'll know that.' He laughed and Ellen smiled again, then cut off the smile as Tess glared at her. 'I was the perfect gentleman,' he told Ellen. 'I put your inebriated daughter on the bed and walked away. She may wish I hadn't but . . .'

'Oh,' Tess raged, groping for something to throw at him. Her hand fell on a fat china cat which she had won at a fair during a village fête; she flung it and Steve ducked. The cat smashed with a good deal of noise; splinters flew in all directions. 'Call yourself a gentleman?' Tess snarled.

'You showed no sign of wanting me to go,' Steve said in a soft purr, then glanced down. 'You'd better get a broom and sweep up the mess before someone cuts themselves on one of those pieces—sharp as a knife, some of them.'

'I hope that wasn't something Hal was fond of,' Ellen said reproachfully. 'This isn't your house, Tess, that was very naughty of you.'

Steve grinned and Tess ignored him. 'It was my cat,' she said. 'It wasn't Hal's, and I'm sorry I lost my temper, Mother.'

'So I should think,' said Steve complacently.

'I wasn't talking to you!'

'It was me you threw the cat at!'

'I wish it had hit you!'

'Children, children,' Ellen lamented softly. 'If you were five years old, I'd smack you both. Tess, go into the kitchen and make some coffee. Steve, come with me into the sitting-room.' She walked away, taking Steve with her. He grinned back at Tess, deliberately needling her, obviously pleased to watch her mother giving her orders that Tess couldn't refuse to obey. Over her shoulder, Ellen said, 'And Tess, do sweep up the broken china, won't you?' and Steve's grin widened.

Tess put her tongue out at Steve who said very loudly, 'It's rude to stick your tongue out, isn't it, Mrs Linden?'

'Tell tale tit,' Tess said, going into the kitchen and banging the door. She began to make coffee, fuming. She wondered exactly what they were saying to each other in the sitting-room—would

Ellen manage to persuade Steve not to go ahead with his warts-and-all biography? Why had he come back? Why had Anna come to the villa? Was she involved in the conspiracy or not; was it all Steve's idea? Tess had a hundred questions to which she wanted an answer, as fast as she thought of one another popped into her head. She went out again to clear the table and then swept the floor and dropped the broken pieces of china cat into the waste bin with a resounding clatter. She wasn't particularly fond of the cat but she hated pointless waste and felt stupid as she dropped the bin lid on its remains. 'Sorry, Pussy,' she muttered, turning away to wash her hands, surprised to see that one piece had scratched her thumb, which was bleeding. She hadn't noticed at the time; the cat had managed to get its own back, she thought, running cold water over the thumb.

When she carried the tray of coffee into the sitting-room, Steve was standing by the stone hearth, his elbow on the wide stone shelf above it while he talked, facing Ellen, who was sitting on the white couch. Behind Steve's black head a tall vase of wild poppies nodded, their silky scarlet petals holding centres of dusty black which, like mascara, came off if you touched it. Tess had picked them along the lane; they would soon drop their petals, of course, but they gave the room a blazing vitality, their colour a splash of blood against the stark white of the wall.

Tess put the tray down on the coffee table and knelt beside it to pour a cup for her mother. She hadn't managed to catch any of their conversation; they had stopped speaking the minute she opened the door.

'Black?' she asked Steve, who nodded.

'And no sugar,' he said, as she had remembered he would.

She handed him a cup and then poured her own, curling up on the floor beside the couch, nursing her cup, looking enquiringly at Ellen.

'Steve has offered to let Johnny read the text before it goes to the publisher,' Ellen said cheerfully, smiling at Steve over her daughter's head.

Tess gave him a surprised look, then frowned. 'And what if he changes the text after Johnny has seen it? Wouldn't it be wiser if Johnny saw the text after it has been copy-edited and before it goes to the printer? With the understanding that if he doesn't like anything, it comes out?'

'Don't be difficult, Tess,' Ellen said.

'That's like asking a cat not to hunt mice,' said Steve. 'This female was born difficult.' He bent over, his jaw set in stubborn lines. 'I'm writing a critical biography, not a piece of hype. I'm sure my publisher's legal eagles will make certain I don't run them into a libel suit. I won't print anything I can't fully substantiate, and I promise you I won't go to any lengths to savage Johnny. But I must have some freedom to show the real man behind the public image—otherwise I don't want to write it at all.'

'Even better!' Tess approved.

Steve eyed her derisively. 'I'm writing this

book at your father's invitation, remember. It was not my idea in the first place—it was his.'

'He didn't think you'd write a debunking book on him!'

'He thought I'd make him out to be some sort of saint, you mean? Well, he was mistaken in the sort of writer I am,' Steve informed her implacably.

'Use one word I've said to you, and I'll kick up hell,' she promised.

'You see what I'm up against?' Steve appealed to Ellen, who was watching them both intently without saying anything.

'Tess and her father have a love-hate relationship,' Ellen said quietly, smiling. 'From the time she hit her teens she has been having a running battle with Johnny, but although she infuriates him he still loves her very much.'

Tess flushed to her hairline. 'News to me!' she muttered, then, catching Steve's thoughtful stare said aggessively to him, 'And this is all off the record—get that! You dare print any of it!'

Steve didn't answer her, he looked at Ellen with a wry smile. 'Do you know what your daughter said to me this morning? She said she was proud of her father, he was a great man and she loved him. I can't say I was amazed; I'd begun to suspect that, for all her apparent hostility to him, she was still deeply attached to him. But I think she was surprised, weren't you, Tess? I think you opened your mouth and said it without realising it was what you really felt.'

'Don't you try to analyse me,' Tess seethed,

her face hot. 'If I want to find out what makes me tick I'll pay a shrink, I don't want any amateur Freuds poking around among my brains.'

'What brains?' Steve mocked. 'Any you have seem to be permanently addled. I have a better idea what makes you tick than you'll ever have. I'd demonstrate but I don't think you'd like to have your mother as an audience.'

Tess shot to her feet, trembling with rage and confusion. 'Go and pack your case and join Anna Cadogan at the Eden-Roc; you won't get any more out of me.'

'Vixen,' Steve said, strolling to the door. 'I was going to leave anyway; you'll have a house full with your mother here.'

The door closed on his lean figure and Tess sat down on the couch before her legs gave under her. Ellen gazed at her mildly.

'What a very explosive relationship you seem to have with him. How long have you known him?'

'What?' Tess was bewildered by the question; it felt like a hundred years since she first set eyes on Steve and she couldn't believe it as she realised how short a time ago it was since she saw the imprint of his body on her bed and realised that a stranger had been in the villa. 'A few days,' she said dazedly. 'That's all. A few days.'

'I'm glad I like him,' Ellen said irrelevantly and Tess stared at her in bafflement.

'Why?'

'I haven't liked any of the other men you've got mixed up with.'

'I am not mixed up with Steve Houghton!' Tess denied hotly.

'I'm very fond of Deirdre, too,' Ellen said with equal irrelevance. 'When you and Hal were small I used to worry sometimes in case you grew up and married someone I couldn't like. Silly really, but family is so important. I'd have hated to be separated from either you or Hal. I hoped you'd both pick someone I could like and feel comfortable with.'

'I'm not planning on marrying Steve Houghton, Mother!' Tess said crossly, very pink.

'Of course not, dear,' Ellen said casually. 'I was just thinking aloud.'

'Well, don't even think it! Not a chance, never in this world. I'd rather marry E.T.'

'Who?' Ellen looked blank.

'You know,' Tess said, then caught her mother's eye and shrugged. 'Well, never mind— just get it through your head; it won't be Steve Houghton.'

'What won't?' his voice said and Tess stiffened, turning her head and trying to control the wave of angry colour rushing up her face.

'Have you packed that case yet?'

'Yes,' he said drily. 'Want to check it to make sure I haven't stolen anything valuable?'

Tess nearly told him that he had, she already knew that, but her heart had no real value—if it had any, she wouldn't have given it so easily to a guy like Steve Houghton who certainly wouldn't look after it. She stared at him, trying to think of something devastating to say, something to wipe the mocking smile off his handsome face—but her mind wasn't co-operating today. She could only think of one thing she wanted to say to him, so she said that.

'Goodbye.'

It had seemed a pretty lame thing to say, but to her surprise it got a violent effect—Steve's eyes flashed like summer lightning under the jagged upward sweep of his dark brows. They looked at each other across the room in a brief, intense battle of wills—Tess couldn't put a name to what she felt or what she read in his eyes, but it came down to just that. It was a fight; silent, bitter, unyielding. Tess felt herself tremble from head to foot, then Steve turned and walked out without another word. She felt like the victor of a ruthless civil war; as much was lost as had been gained and too much had been sacrificed, she would never recover.

CHAPTER NINE

TESS drove Ellen to the airport two days later, in sweltering heat, the sky arching above them like hot blue glass and the sun so fierce it burnt the eyes merely to look upwards. Tess wore dark sunglasses; she was pale under her tan and perspiration dewed her forehead. There seemed to be no breath of air, the palm trees stood still, their shade a spilt pool of black ink around their base.

'You've got your ticket and your passport?' she checked as she turned into the terminal driveway. Nice airport was as crowded as ever; cars came and went, people jostled each other around the entrance, gendarmes in blue shirt sleeves mingled with them, shouting at drivers to move on and trying to keep the human traffic in motion as it flowed in and out of the terminal.

'Don't fret so much,' Ellen said, smiling.

'I'll find somewhere to park and come and see you off,' Tess promised as she drew into the kerb to let Ellen out. She got out, too, and went round to get her mother's case from the boot.

'No, don't,' Ellen said. 'I can manage and the car park looks full.' She took the case from Tess, kissed her cheek. 'It's been lovely to see you. I'll give your love to Hal and Deirdre and the children.' Her eyes teased. 'And to your father.'

Tess laughed wryly. 'You think I'm a crazy mixed-up kid, don't you?'

'I think you're just beginning to grow up,' Ellen said and walked away into the airport. She turned to wave once before she vanished out of sight, and Tess waved back, trying to smile. There was no reason why she should feel like crying—she would see her mother again in a week or so, but then that was not what was making her emotionally tense. Ellen was too perceptive. She had put into words what Tess, herself, had barely realised until now. Her mother was quite right— the last week had made some enormous changes in the way she saw things—herself, her parents, her past and present and even her future. A week ago she would have laughed at the mere suggestion that she was not fully mature. She was only now beginning to understand that she had been trapped in deeply entrenched attitudes for years—kept in a state of angry rebellion which was close to being a permanent adolescence.

A gendarme waved imperiously at her, shouting orders in terse French. Tess hurriedly climbed back into her car and edged her way out of the airport traffic into the complicated one-way system of Nice streets, leaving behind her the curving stretch of the Promenade des Anglaises with its white hotel façades and palm trees above the blue arc of the Baie des Anges. Nice was always thick with traffic; it took her half-an-hour to reach Grasse but once she was past it she reached Vence quite quickly.

She heard Dottie and Franco laughing in the

swimming pool as she went into the villa and decided to join them. It was too hot to do anything else. She went up to her room and changed into a white bikini; her skin much more tanned now after a week of South of France sunshine. Dottie trod water as Tess appeared on the side of the pool.

'You're back! I didn't hear the car. Your mother caught her plane okay?'

'In plenty of time,' Tess said, dropping her towel and sunglasses into one of the loungers and putting a bottle of suntan oil and a book on the table beside it. She ran over to the pool and leapt into the water, the splash sending Dottie a wave of blue water which made her swim away, coughing.

'Hey, watch it!' she called as Tess surfaced.

'Sorry,' Tess said, laughing. She shook her wet hair back from her face with a sigh of relief at the coolness of the water on her hot skin; she felt as if she were drinking the water in at every pore. The heat was dehydrating, she had been sweating freely as she drove back, her clothes had been sticking to her and she had had to peel them off when she changed.

'That's better,' she said. 'My God, it's hot today! It must be the hottest day of the year. You could fry an egg on the pavement in Nice.'

'It was a hundred and five in the shade at noon,' Franco said. 'We've been in the pool for hours. Too hot to do anything else.'

'Did you have lunch?' asked Dottie and Tess grimaced.

'I couldn't eat! It's much too hot.'

'Same here—Franco thought we might have dinner at the Eden-Roc,' Dottie said with a casual air that didn't fool Tess for an instant. Stiffening, Tess shook her head, her mouth wry.

'Not me. I think I'll have an early night—but you two must go, don't worry about me. I've got a lot of sleep to catch up on.' Nothing would coax her into going to the Eden-Roc; wild horses wouldn't drag her there. The last thing she wanted was to see Steve, especially as she suspected that she might see Anna Cadogan there too.

Franco and Dottie exchanged glances of which Tess was perfectly aware. She swam away from them without a backward look, the water rippling along her body like warm silk. Even if she hadn't been afraid of seeing Steve she wouldn't want to turn their duo into a trio—they seemed to be so well matched, she couldn't remember seeing Dottie so happy, Tess did not want to wreck their evening.

It wasn't until six o'clock that the heat showed any sign of diminishing. Tess wandered back to the villa and changed into a pair of shorts and a halter top. Dottie followed her and came into her room as she was brushing her damp hair in front of the dressing-table mirror. She sat down on the bed and Tess eyed her in the glass.

'Tess, we'd like you to join us, you know—you don't have to feel like a gooseberry.' Dottie gazed at her anxiously and Tess smiled, shrugging.

'I do need an early night, thanks all the same.'

'Steve won't be there,' Dottie ventured uncertainly and Tess went on brushing her hair, her hand very steady because she refused to let it tremble.

'No? How can you be sure of that?'

'He's going to a party in Monte Carlo,' Dottie said, shifting uneasily on the bed, rather flushed.

'With Anna Cadogan,' Tess stated drily, a corkscrew of jealousy twisting inside her. She was proud of the fact that it didn't show on her face; she was watching herself, not Dottie, holding her features rigidly in a calm expression. Maybe she should have gone on the stage, she thought, she might have more of her father's talent than she had ever suspected.

'With friends,' Dottie prevaricated, even more unhappy now, and her concern made Tess smile naturally, a rueful appreciation in her face. Dottie had a kind heart, she was upset because she was afraid that Tess was unhappy, and Dottie knew all about the emotional battering men could inflict. Tess had never been in this state before, she had always refused to allow herself to be vulnerable to this sort of sickness, but Dottie had always been more reckless. She had learnt long ago to bounce back; Tess wished now that she had as much experience.

How long does it take to get over it? she wanted to ask Dottie, but she had always been secretive about her feelings. She couldn't break the habit of a lifetime now. She had never been able to discuss how she really felt with anyone, even her own mother—perhaps especially not her mother. Ellen had never talked about her feelings with Tess, and that silence had taught Tess to be silent, too. One could argue forever over which was strongest—heredity or environment. One couldn't argue when both combined. She was her mother's daughter and she found it hard to admit her own emotions. She wished she could break through her self-imposed barrier and ask Dottie how to cope with this endless ache of feeling, but Dottie had always fallen out of love as fast as she fell into it. She might not have any useful advice to give.

'I'm furious with Franco because he didn't tell me about her,' Dottie broke out, staring at their dual reflection in the mirror. 'I'd asked him if Steve had anyone else and Franco swore he hadn't. I might have remembered the way men stick together; their old buddy act makes me sick.'

'Franco probably didn't know about it,' Tess said fair-mindedly. She didn't want to wreck Dottie's relationship with Franco. 'Steve and Anna Cadogan split up once—now they're back together, apparently.'

'I hate to see you so down,' Dottie said agitatedly. 'You're always so level-headed. Oh, men are the living end!'

Tess laughed. 'I'll feel better tomorrow when I've had a good night's sleep. I'm tired—this heat is killing.'

'Okay,' Dottie said, giving in. 'You get an early night, then, and we'll talk about it tomorrow.' She got up and wandered over to the door. 'See you later.'

When Dottie and Franco had driven off, Tess made herself a light snack of fruit and some salad, drank some Perrier, ice-cold from the fridge, then went upstairs to bed after listening to a record for a while. She felt her eyes getting sleepy, her lids too heavy, she kept yawning. It was pointless to sit there going to sleep when she could do it more comfortably in bed. She fell asleep almost at once, her body relaxed in total abandonment without even a sheet covering her because the night was so hot.

When she woke up again it was still dark. She hadn't woken naturally, though; something had startled her awake. A noise? she thought, sitting up on one elbow to peer at her alarm clock. It was only just midnight. She had been asleep for four hours. Had Dottie just come home? Was that what had woken her?

Tess sat up listening for a few moments and was about to lie down again when a very recognisable noise made her jump. It was a splash, a loud splash. Someone had just dived into the swimming pool.

Tess stumbled out of bed, groping for her thin cotton wrap. What on earth was Dottie up to? It was still intensely hot, the air seemed to smoulder as it touched her bare skin, but Dottie was swimming so noisily. Didn't she realise she might wake people up? Had she brought Franco back with her? Were they drunk, for heaven's sake?

Tess crossly ran downstairs and out into the garden; a full moon had risen and was silvering the trees and bushes, making ghostly the tall, white lilies. She did not need a torch to see her way towards the pool; the garden was like a lit stage with black shadows pressing around the periphery.

By that strange light she saw the sleek black head cruising through the water. For a second her heart stopped and she didn't seem to be breathing, then pure rage exploded inside her head, and she began to run, shaking with a desire to do violence to someone, preferably Steve.

'What the hell do you think you're doing in there?' she yelled as she reached the side of the pool, and Steve's head turned lazily in her direction, but he didn't slow his pace or answer her. Moonlight glimmered on his bare brown shoulders and the arm curving up out of the water. She saw the glittering drops fall back into the blue pool as the spray he was sending up descended again.

'Are you deaf?' Tess demanded. 'How dare you stroll into my garden and use my pool without permission. This is private property. What do you think you're doing?'

'Swimming?' he drawled, streaking past, and the mockery made her teeth clench.

'Come out before I call the police!' she threatened.

He had reached the other end of the pool and turned in a smooth sliding movement which gave her a glimpse of his muscled chest, the damp black hair growing down the centre of it.

'This is the hottest night of the year so far,' he informed her as he swam back towards her.

'I don't want to discuss the weather—I just want you to leave!' Tess seethed impotently. How did you force a man to get out of a swimming pool? What did the gardener use to skim floating leaves and other debris from the surface of the pool? A rake, wasn't it? Tess glanced at the garden hut yearningly but was afraid of threatening him with the rake. It might turn into a farcical battle.

'A pool is as good a place as any to spend the night,' Steve told her as he turned and came back. 'Unless you have an alternative suggestion?'

'Get out of that pool!' Tess commanded, stamping her bare foot. That was a mistake, she suddenly realised, with a stab of alarm, because the edge of the pool was wet and slippery and before she could stop herself she felt her feet skidding under her and with her arms waving desperately in an attempt to regain her balance she lunged forward and toppled into the pool.

She struggled back to the surface to find herself confronting Steve who gave her a satisfied smile. 'I hoped you'd join me,' he told her and Tess, spluttering and winded, could hardly breathe for fury.

'You . . . you . . .' she stuttered and he eyed her teasingly.

'Leave you speechless, do I? That's a good sign.' He moved closer and she felt his hands at her waist.

'Don't you touch me!' Tess reacted shakily, slapping the hands away.

'I was going to take off your robe, you can't swim in that.'

Tess had already realised as much but then she didn't intend to do any swimming, she was getting out of the pool right now. She turned back to the side and grabbed the wet tiles with both hands to pull herself up out of the water. Steve's arm coiled snakelike round her waist and jerked her backwards, kicking and struggling.

'Let go ...' she began and found herself floating on her back with Steve's head between her and the moon. His face was dark and shadowy but the gleam of his eyes made her shake.

He smiled down at her as she lay still, her body buoyed up on the warm water, her hands on his shoulders, her fingers clenched on his bare skin.

'I thought I told you I never wanted to see you again,' she whispered, wishing her heart would stop beating so hard her body shook with the reverberations.

Steve undid the belt of her wrap and the wet material floated away, leaving her in nothing but a brief lawn nightdress which clung to her body like a second, but completely transparent skin.

As his eyes flashed down over her Tess shuddered, stammering, 'Don't!' Don't look at me, she meant, but she was too breathless to get the rest of the sentence out. She was too late to stop him, anyway; Steve was staring at her and if he was acting the desire she saw in those dark-pupilled eyes he had more talent than her father. Her mouth went dry, her breasts ached with a fierce inflow of blood that made them round and lift, her nipples hardening and showing stiffly through the clinging wet material.

'Tess,' he said huskily, his fingers moving to encircle one breast, his thumb softly caressing the outlined nipple.

His head lowered and she stared achingly at the warm line of his mouth, wanting to kiss it so much that she didn't even try to push him away, she met his kiss hungrily, her arms going round his neck.

Steve's hands lifted her in the water, her feet touched the bottom, their wet bodies clung as she slid down against him, her breasts against his naked chest and her thighs caught between his parted legs. Her eyes closed as the urgent power of his body overwhelmed her, the instinctive female reaction to submit so strong that her rational mind couldn't fight it.

His hands moved everywhere, igniting the passion she would have tried to douse, and she wondered how he knew exactly where to touch her so that he undermined all her resistance. She briefly hated those expert hands, that coaxing mouth—what other women had taught him such damnable skill?

Water rippled against her and she woke from her trance of pleasure to realise that Steve was wading through the pool, carrying her breast high. Her eyes opened and she looked up at his moonlit face, seeing it cearly now, and shaken by the taut lines of jaw and cheekbone. She recognised that tension, felt it inside herself, it was the agonising nag of desire that set his face.

He lifted her slight body effortlessly on to the tiled surround of the pool, and a second later heaved himself out, water streaming from his bare chest. Tess scrambled to her feet at that instant, trembling, backing in an atavistic fear of the aroused male, her eyes wide and her face pale in the moonlight.

Steve faced her, breathing audibly. For a second they were in silent conflict, locked in an age-old confrontation for which there were no words. Tess was deaf and blind to everything but the imminent threat of the muscled male body a step away from her, then Steve seemed to break free of his own brief uncertainty. He took a stride and with a smothered gasp of alarm Tess turned and fled back to the house, hearing him coming behind her. Both barefoot they ran through the moonlit garden, the bushes and trees breathing softly like a fascinated audience. Tess felt her own breath coming hard and impeded, heard Steve's breathing far too close, coming closer.

Her hand fumbled for the door handle, she didn't wait to shut it, she ran through the silent house, her steps slithering on the tiled floor.

'Be careful,' Steve gasped behind her as she almost fell on the open staircase and the sound of his voice made her put on more speed.

He caught her on the landing before she reached her bedroom door. His arms closed round her like iron bars, welding her body to his own. Tess heaved and struggled, fighting as if for her life, and felt his mouth heatedly moving on the nape of her neck, pushing aside the wet strands of hair, sliding down her throat.

'No, Steve,' she moaned, straining against the immovable barrier which held her locked to him.

'I love you,' he muttered into her ear, his tongue silky as it followed the convolutions of the whorled pink skin.

'No!' she denied, refused to believe. The lie made her angry, she twisted and tossed inside the imprisoning arms, her own longing to believe making her violent. She wouldn't be caught that way, she wouldn't be trapped and deceived.

Steve picked her up so suddenly that she hadn't expected and couldn't counter the movement. He carried her into her bedroom and laid her on the bed, kneeling over her, framing her rebellious face within his hands, his powerful body holding her down as she fought to escape.

'Look at me!'

Tess shut her eyes, her mouth a bitter, resisting line. His fingers were warm on her damp face, the palms enclosing her cheeks, curving in with them as if they belonged where they lay.

Steve's mouth gently brushed her mouth. 'I love you,' he said again. 'I didn't expect it, it just happened, I must have a weakness for small spitting cats with angry eyes that have a funny sad look when they think no one is watching. You make me feel weak, Tess, weak inside; I want to look after you, make you smile all the time instead of only when you forget to scowl.'

Tess pretended she wasn't hearing any of that.

she kept her lids down and her mouth closed and unyielding.

'You don't believe me now, but you will,' Steve said in that husky voice.

Tess knew she wouldn't, never could believe him. Men like Steve didn't fall in love with girls like her; they fell for sexy girls with red hair and fabulous figures, like Anna Cadogan, and remembering the other woman made her open her eyes and look at him icily.

'Go back to Anna Cadogan,' she said with the lance of pain in her voice.

'Darling,' Steve said, his mouth curving warmly. 'You don't need to be jealous of Anna, of anyone.'

Her face burned. 'Jealous? I'm not jealous of anyone,' she said. 'Jealous over you? I've got more self-respect. You arrived here, deliberately intending to wheedle information out of me to use to hurt my father. You're a fake and a liar.'

He sighed, his face set in wry, defensive lines. 'Do we have to talk about that?' Their eyes met and Steve shrugged, the wet skin rippling over his broad shoulders. 'Okay, we'll talk about that now but I could think of more enjoyable things to do.' He slid off her and lay down, one arm over her to hold her on the bed.

'You're right, of course. That was my original intention. I was angry with Johnny and I decided it was time someone wrote the truth about him. The gossip columns revel in his private life, they never seem to wonder what he does to the women he gets involved with.'

Tess lay on her back, staring bitterly at the ceiling. 'Anna Cadogan, for example,' she said coldly.

'Yes,' Steve admitted. 'But it wasn't so much that he took Anna from me, because I'd got over that months ago. You were right when you said that if Anna had been in love with me she wouldn't have dropped me for Johnny—and if I'd been in love with Anna I wouldn't have got over her so fast, that's just as true. We were never right for each other, I enjoyed her company and she's very attractive, but there's that extra something that makes for strong sexual attraction and Anna and I never had that.'

Tess felt her heart beating against her breastbone, so strongly that she felt sick. Was he telling the truth? She was afraid to believe him; she wanted it to be true too much.

'What made me violently angry was discovering that Johnny had dropped Anna once the play ended its run. It seemed so callous, so cold-blooded. He'd done that before, too many times. People started telling me about all the other times, they seemed to think it would make me feel better to know how often Johnny Linden had moved in on his latest leading lady, how many times he'd broken up other men's love lives.' Steve sighed. 'Maybe if I hadn't been writing this damned biography of him I'd have listened to them and realised Johnny's behaviour was a pattern and a habit, and then forgotten all about it—but I was being asked to write about his character, his life story, and I was angry enough to think I ought to write the unvarnished truth about him.'

'If you hadn't still cared about Anna Cadogan, you wouldn't have been so angry,' Tess said in a very quiet voice, trying to sound neutral when she didn't feel in the least neutral. On the contrary, she cared too much.

Steve rolled on to his side and looked into her face. 'Darling, it was my own ego I cared about. Johnny had snatched my toy away and I wanted to smack him.' He grinned at her. 'And that's the unnattractive truth about *me*—I lost my temper. He hadn't hurt me, he had annoyed me.'

Tess believed him and wasn't in the least relieved or comforted. So that was how he thought about women, was it? They were toys for men to fight over. That fitted Johnny's attitude, too; when he was bored with his latest toy he chucked it out of his playpen and bellowed for something new. After all, toys don't have feelings. They don't matter.

'Does Anna know she was just your newest toy?' she asked remotely. 'That might explain why she cheerfully walked away to Johnny. I don't know that I blame her.'

'I said it was unattractive,' Steve pleaded in his own defence.

And that makes it okay, does it? I'm supposed to be disarmed immediately by your appealing honesty.'

'Shrew,' he said trying to kiss her, and Tess tossed her head to one side, giving him her frozen profile to admire.

'How did you know I would be at Hal's villa? Anna?'

'Yes,' he said. 'I met her at a party a couple of nights before I flew over here—she was quite cheerful on the surface but several of the women went out of their way to make spiteful jokes at her expense and Anna didn't like that.'

'Who would?' Tess thought aloud, feeling faint sympathy for the first time. She knew the sort of women who made those sort of jokes. She had suffered at their hands herself.

'I didn't ask her about Johnny at first, I tried to stay off the subject, but Anna mentioned that she had stayed at Johnny's villa in the South of France and said she must remember to give him back the key because the last time she saw him he had said his daughter was going there for a couple of weeks. That was when I got the idea. I remembered the villa, Johnny had told me I could borrow it any time I liked—maddening though he is, he can be very generous.'

'It isn't his villa,' Tess muttered.

'I didn't know that,' Steve said impatiently. 'I thought it was and I asked Anna to give me the key, said I'd give it back to him and ask if I could borrow it to do some research for his biography. She knew I was working on it, she didn't guess what was in my head.'

Tess threw him a scathing, incredulous look. 'Do you honestly expect me to believe that?'

'Why do you think she turned up here the other day? Johnny got in touch with her, in a panic, and asked her to intervene—persuade me not to use any damaging material in the book. Anna drove over here to do just that. She wasn't in any plot with me. She's too generous-minded, she's quite tolerant about Johnny now. I gather the end of the affair was amicable, a mutual decision. She bears him no ill will, in fact I'd say she's rather fond of him. I don't know what the man's got but women seem to forgive him anything.' Steve sounded irritated and Tess glanced at him out of the corner of her eye, seeing his hard mouth indented.

'He has charm,' she said, thinking that Johnny wasn't the only one. Steve had charm, too, and used it as ruthlessly. He had a lot in common with her father and it wasn't the first time she had realised as much. She had known it the second she set eyes on him but her foresight and intuition hadn't saved her from making a calamitous fool of herself. She should have gone ahead and sent for the police, boarded herself up inside the villa behind a hedge of thorns, kept Steve away by any means in her power. Then she might have been safe.

'Yes,' Steve said drily. 'Anna had told me a little about you, enough to give me a clue to how you felt about your father. I hoped you'd hand me plenty of inside information. From what I'd heard about you, it seemed on the cards that you would want to hit back at him too.'

'You expected me to be an ally, a fellow conspirator.' Tess watched the brown edge of his profile with that aching awareness she was beginning to recognise with despair. She

wondered if she really wanted to be safe—
sometimes safety can be more dangerous than
danger itself. What sort of life did you have, walled
up securely where love could not reach you?

'Exactly. I hadn't expected to find myself with
such a fight on my hands. Women are irrational
creatures. You weren't what I imagined I'd find.
You obviously had a crazy love-hate relationship
with your father but at the same time I had to
winkle every tiny bit of information out of you.
You were suspicious and touchy and I could see
you had been badly scarred by whatever you felt
about Johnny.'

'It isn't easy being his daughter,' Tess said
flatly. 'Everyone used to look at me as if I was
a changeling—Johnny's so unbelievably good-
looking, and I'm so plain.'

'You are *not* plain!' Steve said, arching over her
and touching her cheek with one gentle hand.
Tess avoided his eyes, her skin hot.

'Don't lie to me, I know what I see when I look
into a mirror. I'm skinny and plain.'

'Never mind mirrors,' Steve said softly. 'Look
into my eyes. Then you'll see what I see.'

'No,' Tess said defiantly, looking away, her lids
down and her lashes flickering in agitation
against her flushed cheek. She would not let
Steve hypnotise her into believing lies.

'Tess,' he said, his fingers travelling over her
tense face as if he was a blind man discovering
her by touch; his cool light fingertips moulding
her forehead, nose, eyes, cheeks, stubborn jaw,
making her shiver with awareness. 'That night we

were at the Eden-Roc and I got you drunk ...'

'Deliberately!'

'Yes,' he admitted. 'I intended to make you talkative, I thought it would loosen your tongue—instead you went to sleep and then I started wanting you. I had quite a tussle with my conscience before I walked out of this room that night. When I kissed you I found I'd caught a little wild cat; I hadn't guessed you were so passionate.'

'Stop it!' she protested, squirming.

He laughed huskily. 'Why don't you want to admit it? You went to my head that night. I've been waiting ever since to do it again.'

'Not with me!' Tess assured him, her slender body tense. 'I'm not available—I didn't inherit my father's taste for promiscuity any more than I inherited his looks.'

'I'm relieved to hear it,' Steve said with dry emphasis. 'Now can we forget about Johnny?'

'How can we do that? You're still writing that book and I'd be a fool if I trusted you after listening to what you just told me. You don't honestly expect me to trust you?'

'I've been thinking hard ever since you chucked me out of here the other day,' he said wryly. 'I've changed my mind. I won't use a word of anything I picked up from you or your mother. I've decided to write the book the way Johnny wants it written. The biographers who come after me can uncover the real Johnny Linden—I'll just write about his career and skate over his private life.'

Tess stared at him warily. 'Why? What changed your mind?'

'You did,' Steve said, smiling. 'If I wrote the book I intended to write I'd lose any chance with you, wouldn't I?' He watched the slow flush climb her face, his eyes alert. 'My thirst for revenge died a natural death three days ago—you matter far more to me than doing a hatchet job on Johnny. I liked him a lot until he went after Anna, you know. You were right, he has charm, damn him—but most importantly, he's your father. I thought I was being very clever, coming here to find you. I didn't expect it to change my whole life.'

Tess looked down, her throat beating with a hot pulse of excitement. She was still afraid to trust him, but what if he meant what he had just said? What if she was refusing a real emotion because she was so scared of being given counterfeit?

She watched him through her lowered lashes, startled as if for the first time by those hard-boned good looks. Could he really be attracted to anyone as ordinary as her?

'How did you know I'd be here alone tonight?' she asked, suddenly wondering.

'Franco told me,' he said, his mouth crooked with angry amusement. 'He's been keeping me informed about your movements!' His eyes mocked her.

'Spying on me!' she said, trying to stay angry.

'Needing to hear about you,' Steve corrected softly. 'I love you,' he said again and each time he said it, it seemed more possible and she liked the sound of it more. If he said it every hour on the hour, like a cuckoo clock, in a hundred years she might actually believe it.

She looked into those silvery eyes to find the reflection he had promised she would see and her body trembled at what his gaze showed her. She didn't see herself so much as Steve's desire for her and that was heady enough to weaken all her defences. He saw it and his mouth curved in a tender, aroused warmth; his hand moved down her body and she closed her eyes, lifting her mouth.

She wasn't going to tell him how she felt, not yet; she needed the conviction of his lips, the powerful arguments of his body, before she would be ready to make any admission of her own emotions, but they had all night, there was no hurry, tomorrow need never come for them until this first wild rush of passion had been sated.

'Oh, Tess,' Steve groaned in a weakness she had never expected from him and then, for the first time, she began to glimpse the truth of what they could mean to each other. As his body trembled with that urgent need of her she closed her arms around him and was complete; no longer afraid to love or to give herself and accepting Steve's gift of himself without doubts. In a minute she would tell him she loved him, she thought, and then she stopped thinking and there was no need for words.

Coming Next Month in Harlequin Presents!

847 LION OF DARKNESS Melinda Cross
The New York doctor, who's helped so many cope with blindness in a sighted world, is baffled by his latest case—and a force that threatens the doctor–patient relationship.

848 THE ARROGANT LOVER Flora Kidd
A young widow distrusts the man who tries to come between her and her Scottish inheritance. He made love to her, then left without a word nine years ago. Why should she trust him now?

849 GIVE ME THIS NIGHT Vanessa James
Passion flares between a tour guide and a mystery writer on the Greek island of Paxos. But she's blundered into his life at the worst possible moment—because around him, she senses danger!

850 EXORCISM. Penny Jordan
Once she naively assumed he'd marry her if they made love. Now he wants her to help him research his new book in the Caribbean. Why? To exorcise the past?

851 SLEEPING DESIRE Charlotte Lamb
After a year apart, can an estranged wife forget the solicitor's letters and the divorce proceedings? Easily—when the man she loves reawakens her desire.

852 THE DEVIL'S PRICE Carole Mortimer
The day she left him, their love turned to ashes. But a London singer is willing to bargain with the devil to be with her lover again—but not as his wife!

853 SOUTH SEAS AFFAIR Kay Thorpe
Against her better judgment, against all her values, a young woman allows herself to be drawn into a passionate affair with her father's archenemy!

854 SUN LORD'S WOMAN Violet Winspear
Fate, which seemed to have been so kind, deals a cruel blow to a young woman on her wedding night, and her husband's desert kingdom loses its dreamlike appeal.

Take 4 best-selling love stories FREE
Plus get a FREE surprise gift!

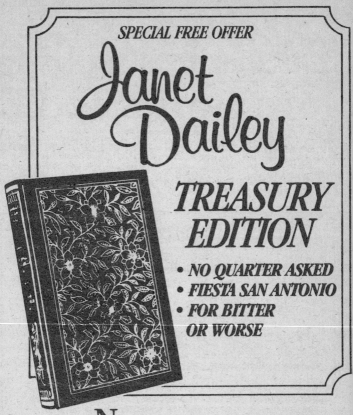

Here's how to get this special offer from Harlequin!
As simple as 1...2...3!

1. Each month, save one Treasury Edition coupon from your favorite Romance or Presents novel.
2. In four months you'll have saved four Treasury Edition coupons (<u>only one coupon</u> per month allowed).
3. Then all you have to do is fill out and return the order form provided, along with the four Treasury Edition coupons required and $1.00 for postage and handling.

Mail to: Harlequin Reader Service

In the U.S.A.
2504 West Southern Ave.
Tempe, AZ 85282

In Canada
P.O. Box 2800, Postal Station A
5170 Yonge Street
Willowdale, Ont. M2N 6J3

RT1-E-2

Please send me my FREE copy of the Janet Dailey Treasury Edition. I have enclosed the four Treasury Edition coupons required and $1.00 for postage and handling along with this order form.

(Please Print)

NAME_____

ADDRESS_____

CITY_____

STATE/PROV. _____ ZIP/POSTAL CODE_____

SIGNATURE_____

This offer is limited to one order per household.

SUPPLIES LIMITED

This special Janet Dailey offer expires January 1986.